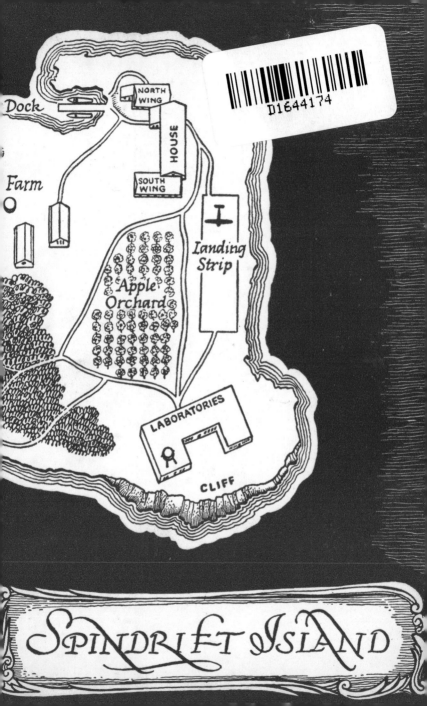

100 FATHOMS UNDER

The Rick Brant Science-Adventure Stories

BY JOHN BLAINE

★

THE ROCKET'S SHADOW
THE LOST CITY
SEA GOLD
100 FATHOMS UNDER

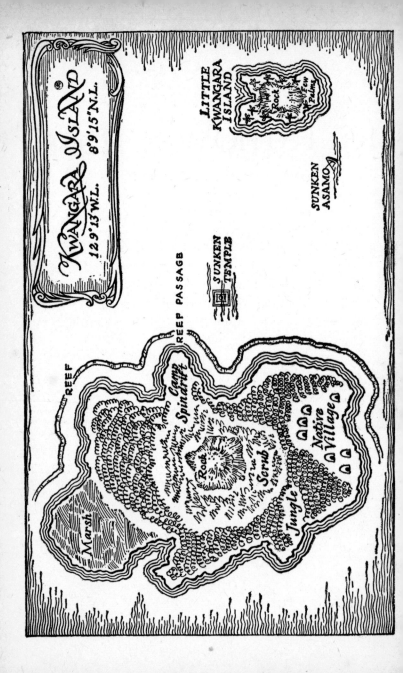

A Rick Brant Electronic Adventure

100 FATHOMS UNDER

by
JOHN BLAINE

SAMPSON LOW
LONDON

© 1947 BY GROSSET & DUNLAP INC

THIS EDITION PUBLISHED PURSUANT TO AGREEMENT WITH
GROSSET & DUNLAP INC., NEW YORK, N.Y., U.S.A.

MADE AND PRINTED IN GREAT BRITAIN BY
PURNELL & SONS, LTD., PAULTON (SOM) AND LONDON

Contents

CHAPTER I

Honolulu!

RICK BRANT looked up from the book he was reading and grinned at the young man across the table. "You look worried, Scotty."

Don Scott was staring through the window at the silvery-blue ocean 10,000 feet below. "Not worried," he said, "just thoughtful. Here we are riding in style a couple of miles above the Pacific. In three weeks we'll be playing tag with the fish a hundred fathoms under it. The trouble with us is, we can't decide whether we want to be birds or porpoises."

Rick put down his book and stretched luxuriously. He was a tall, husky boy of high-school age, with brown hair and eyes. "No bird ever rode in such comfort," he said, glancing around at the lounge of the Pan-American Clipper. "Not much like the Cub, is it?"

He had been gone from home only four days, but already he missed the yellow Piper Cub that was his special pride and joy. He missed Spindrift Island, too. To the rest of the world, the famous island off the New Jersey coast was the headquarters of the Spindrift scientists, led by Hartson W. Brant, Rick's father. The island was known as the place where new radar discoveries had been developed, and as the launching site for the first moon rocket. The very name of Spindrift was synonymous with revolutionary discoveries in the field of electronics. But to Rick, it was simply home. He always hated to leave, even to take part in an exciting scientific expedition like the present one. And he was always glad to return.

"I'm a little homesick," he confessed.

Scotty grinned. "Think you're the only one?" He motioned to two travellers on the opposite side of the lounge. "Take a look at a couple of others."

Rick looked over to where his father and Chahda were seated on a comfortable sofa. Hartson Brant was holding a book, but he wasn't reading. He was staring through the window, lost in thought.

"I'll bet no one aboard realizes who he is," Scotty said.

Rick nodded. His father was known internationally as an outstanding electronic scientist, but it would be hard for a stranger to connect the name of Hartson Brant with the youthful-looking man in the casual slacks and sport jacket. Mr. Brant had his son's lean hardness and unassuming friendliness. More than once he had been mistaken for Rick's older brother. He was an able athlete and an ardent fisherman and swimmer. There was nothing about him to indicate the scientist.

"He's probably thinking about Mom's cooking," Rick said.

"Stop it," Scotty complained. "You're making me hungry. What's Chahda thinking about?"

Seated next to Hartson Brant was a slim brown boy who had a mischievous look about him, even when completely relaxed. Chahda, whom Scotty called "a souvenir of the Tibet trip," was a former Bombay beggar boy who had become a member of the Spindrift family by virtue of his courage and loyalty when the scientists sent an expedition to Tibet to set up a radar moon relay station. The quick-witted Hindu boy had done much to extricate the expedition from serious danger, as related in *The Lost City*.

"He's dreaming about statistics from *The World Almanac*," Rick guessed. He knew that was a safe assumption, because Chahda had been studying a new edition of the *Almanac* that Rick had given him. In Bombay the Hindu boy had tried to educate himself by memorizing most of an old copy of the "Worrold Alm-in-ack," as he called it. It was the only textbook he had had.

Chahda turned suddenly and saw Rick and Scotty watching him. He rose and came across the lounge. "You know what? I am doing some arithmetic."

"With some dope from the *Almanac*?" Rick asked.

Chahda looked surprised. "How you know?"

Rick and Scotty laughed. "Rick's a mind reader," Scotty said. "What are you figuring this time?"

Chahda sat down at the table with them. "We get to Honolulu in one hour, yes? Well, Honolulu is 4,500 miles from Spindrift."

"Which means we've travelled over halfway," Rick added, "because Kwangara is 3,000 miles from Honolulu."

Chahda shook his head. "Is Rick a scientist? No! He is being most careless with numbers. Kwangara is 3,000 miles, yes. But is being ocean miles! That is what I am figuring."

Rick thought for a moment, then he grinned. "You're right," he agreed. "I forgot about the difference between nautical miles and statute miles." He had measured the distance from Spindrift to Kwangara Island, a tiny dot in the Pacific between the Palau Islands and the Southern Philippines, and had got 7,500 miles.

"It says in Alm-in-ack," Chahda stated, "to change to land miles from ocean miles, must multiply by 1.15157."

Scotty shook his head. "This heathen character always amazes me. How can you remember those figures, Chahda?"

Chahda's quick grin flashed. "Is having strong mind. Scotty is opposite. Scotty has strong back, weak mind."

"Think so?" Scotty winked at Rick. "Okay, let's see you solve this problem: A ship leaves New York with twenty men aboard. It goes to London. Two men desert, and the captain hires three more. At Marseille, four men jump overboard and the captain hires two more. The ship goes to Alexandria and the captain hires five men, but two get sick. Got that?"

Chahda had been concentrating. "I got. Now what?"

"At Singapore, they meet pirates and three men are wounded. The captain hires five of the pirates."

"Now you want to know how many men is aboard?" Chahda asked.

"Nope." Scotty grinned. "What's the name of the captain?"

Chahda puzzled for a while, then shrugged. "Give up."

"His name is Jones," Scotty said.

"How you know that?"

Scotty winked at Rick again. "I asked him."

Chahda couldn't decide whether to laugh or not. He compromised by ignoring Scotty. "Anyway, I figure out Kwangara is about 3,800 land miles from Honolulu."

"What does that prove?" Scotty asked.

"I ignoring you," Chahda said with dignity.

Rick smiled. The war between Scotty and Chahda was something that was never ended. They were the best of friends, always willing to fight each other's battles, but equally willing to fight each other between times.

"A few hundred miles on *top* of the ocean doesn't mean much," Rick said. "The distance that counts is straight down. The longest part of the trip is going to be that first long dive in the Submobile."

"Be pretty big adventure," Chahda agreed. "How we know how far down we have to go?"

"We don't," Rick said. "All we have is the estimate of the Pacific Ethnographic Society. They think the temple of Alta-Yuan is in between 500 and 600 feet of water."

"I guess we can take their word for it," Scotty remarked. "I wonder where Professor Zircon and the Submobile are now? We must have passed them."

Rick nodded. "During the night, probably. The *Aloha* is due in Honolulu tomorrow morning." Professor Hobart Zircon was aboard the SS *Aloha* with all the expedition equipment, including the undersea craft they had named the Submobile, and the newly developed Sonoscope underwater search device with which they hoped to salvage part of the sunken temple.

The sixth member of the Spindrift expedition, Professor Gordon, was already in Honolulu. He had arranged for a suitable ship and had done research on the project with the scientists of the Pacific Ethnographic Society, joint sponsors of the expedition.

"This isn't much like our other experiments," Scotty said. "Everything's smooth as velvet."

"Praise be," Rick returned. "Let's have no trouble on this trip."

Bad luck and interference by men who had reasons for wanting the experiments to fail had threatened the success of many of the other Spindrift projects. Rick and Scotty had met during one such period of trouble. Scotty, newly discharged from the Marine Corps, had rescued Rick from a beating at the hands of a gang that was trying to sabotage the Spindrift moon rocket, as related in *The Rocket's Shadow*. Since that time Scotty, an orphan, had made his home with the Spindrift Island group.

"You're getting back into your old territory, Scotty," Rick said. "Going to look up any of your friends?"

Although only one year older than Rick, Scotty had served with the Marines in the Pacific and had been to Hawaii. "My friends are all back in the States," Scotty said. "Besides, we won't have time. We'll just load the equipment and shove off for Kwangara."

Hartson Brant came across the lounge to them. "We're about to land, boys. Honolulu is directly ahead."

Rick looked through the window and saw that the Clipper was already losing altitude. He moved over and made room for his father; then they buckled safety belts and settled down for the landing.

They saw Koko Head come into view, then Diamond Head and Waikiki Beach. They swung low over Honolulu, a modern city of brown and white and green, and splashed to a smooth landing at the Pan-American base between the city and Pearl Harbour. In a few moments they were docked and the steward was opening the doors.

Hartson Brant led the way and Rick followed with a

rising sense of excitement. The first long step of the journey was over!

A short, stocky man with cropped, grey hair came to meet them, and greeted the boys as an old friend. He was Professor John Gordon, a former Navy officer and an expert on aviation electronics and jet propulsion. It was his hobby of archaeology, however, a field in which he was a recognized authority, that had earned him a place on the present trip.

Professor Gordon introduced them to Dr. Paul Warren, a tall, smiling scientist with a neat, brown beard. He was head of the Pacific Ethnographic Society and an old friend of Hartson Brant. Dr. Warren ushered the Spindrift party into his station wagon, and in a few moments they were rolling through the streets of Honolulu.

"Zircon arrives in the morning," Professor Gordon told them. "I've made arrangements with the port authorities to unload at once. We can leave for Kwangara in from three to four days."

"What sort of vessel is the *Tarpon*?" Hartson Brant asked. "You said that she is a trawler in your letter, but you gave no details."

"She'll do nicely," Gordon replied. "She has a steam winch that can handle the Submobile, and a smaller electric winch for the salvage cable. She has a radio-phone and radio direction finder. I've increased her power plant by adding a Diesel generator I got from Navy surplus. We've leased her for three months, with permission to make necessary changes. I've had her holds converted to cabin space and she's repainted from stem to stern."

Dr. Warren chuckled. "You should know in advance, however, that there's something very fishy about her."

Rick stiffened. "How d'you mean, fishy?" he asked quickly.

"Fishy in the most literal sense," Gordon said. In spite of the new paint, there's a faint but definite aroma of long-dead fish about her. You'll get used to it."

"My people have planned a small dinner in honour of your arrival," Dr. Warren said. "It isn't every day we have the famous Spindrift scientists arriving in Honolulu. We'll celebrate at your hotel at seven this evening."

Hartson Brant laughed. "Are you impressed by our past accomplishments, Paul, or are you just flattering us so we'll work harder to dredge up some old bones for you to study?"

"A little of both," Dr. Warren returned with a grin. "But it's a pleasure to see you again, Hartson. I'm looking forward to seeing Hobart Zircon tomorrow, too. It's a long time since our last meeting."

The station wagon crossed a bridge over a small canal and Professor Gordon pointed out into the bay. "See the yachts? This is Kewalo Basin. Our own dock is just around the corner."

Rick looked, but he could see nothing that might have been their trawler. "Where are we staying?" he asked.

"At the Lehra Hotel," Dr. Warren replied. "My own place is too far out of town for convenience, although I'd have liked you to stay with me. Mrs. Warren is getting ready for your mother and sister. I'm afraid she has so much planned they'll be worn out after a month."

"Not Barby," Rick said. "Nothing wears her out. She has more pep than a jumping jack."

Barby Brant, Rick's pretty sister, and his mother were spending a week with relatives on the West Coast before coming to Hawaii by ship to be the guests of Dr. and Mrs. Warren. The feminine members of the Spindrift family would be waiting when the expedition returned to Hawaii.

In a few moments the station wagon swung into a long driveway that led to a building almost hidden by a mass of green, fragrant shrubbery. Hawaiian bellboys came running, smiling a greeting.

The Lehua proved to be a cottage hotel. The guests lived in small cottages set along shaded walks. After registering, Gordon led the way to their quarters. He had arranged for two cottages, side by side, and only a hundred feet from the water. The scientists were to share one cottage while the boys shared the other.

Rick noticed that his father was deep in conversation with Dr. Warren and Professor Gordon. The older members of the party had a lot to talk over. They wouldn't miss the boys.

"Who's for a swim?" he asked.

Scotty and Chahda lost no time in agreeing. They hurried to unpack and get into their suits, then they raced for the water front.

A stone sea wall ran along the front of the hotel grounds, a sandy beach below it. The central path from the cottages ended in an open-air pavilion that was built out over the beach. The water was clear green, the bottom crushed coral.

Rick tested the temperature with his toe. "Not much like Spindrift," he said. "It's pretty warm."

Like all boys away from home, he had the habit of comparing everything with its counterpart at home, and at the moment, the bracing, cool water of the Atlantic seemed better than the warm Pacific.

Chahda stated, "In tropics Alm-in-ack not mentioning icebergs."

"Don't be so literal," Rick said. "I only remarked that it's warm. Well, what are we waiting for?"

"Nothing." Scotty put a period to the word by jumping from the sea wall, taking a short run, and diving into the water. Rick and Chahda were right behind him.

Rick swam along the bottom for a moment, then shot to the surface. "Whee!" he exclaimed. "First swim in the Pacific!" He stood waist-deep in water and looked out past the reef to the open sea. For the first time he felt as though the adventure was really under way. It wouldn't be long before he was exploring the ocean depths from the interior of the Submobile.

Scotty bobbed to the surface like a cork and Chahda splashed in circles, doing his own variation of the dog paddle. The Hindu boy was just learning to swim.

For an hour they enjoyed the famous water of the Waikiki district, Rick and Scotty taking turns in instructing Chahda. Then, tiring of the sport, they sprawled on the warm sand next to the pavilion.

Rick had noticed that two men were seated in the pavilion, but he paid them no attention until he heard Professor Gordon's name mentioned. He turned his head and looked up. The men were seated with their backs to him. One was dressed in a well-cut grey suit. His shoulders were the most prominent thing about him. They were enormous, seeming to push out the material of his coat. He had black hair, cut rather close, and when he spoke his voice was commanding, his words, clipped.

The second man wore stained dungarees and a ragged sweater. He was thin, and almost bald except for a fringe of sandy hair. He spoke in an accent that Rick thought was English.

"Did you get the stuff aboard all right?" the man in the grey suit asked.

"Aye. Soon's you called I got one of the lads and we nipped aboard with it."

"Any trouble?"

"Not any. It's stowed good. Saw to it meself."

"Good. Then we'll be all set when we raise Kwangara. How about the provisions?"

"All stowed proper. I'd best be gettin' back. You comin'?"

"Not now. I have a few things to do."

At the mention of Kwangara, Rick had felt Scotty's hand tighten on his arm. He nodded slightly, indicating that he had heard. He kept an eye on the two men as they rose, lit cigars, and strolled down the boardwalk to the sea wall. Not until they started up the path to the hotel did he see their faces.

The man with the grey suit was swarthy, and his face was almost square, with a tough chin and a firm mouth. His companion had a long, horsey face and eyes that seemed lighter in colour than his skin.

Suddenly the dark man half turned, as though he felt Rick watching him. For an instant, piercing dark eyes locked with Rick's, then the man smiled and nodded and continued up the path to the hotel.

When they were out of hearing, Scotty demanded, "And what was all that?"

"I don't know," Rick answered grimly, "but we're going to find out. Did you get a look at them?"

"That man in grey suit, he is what Scotty calls tough consumer," Chahda declared.

"Tough customer," Scotty corrected. "You're right, Chahda. What do you suppose they were talking about?"

"Horseface took something aboard ship," Rick said thoughtfully. "And since they mentioned Professor Gordon and Kwangara, it must be our ship. We'd better check up. If there's anything off-colour going on, we want to clip it before it gets going good."

"Let's go." Scotty stood up. "Maybe Professor Gordon will have some ideas."

As they hiked up the path, Rick asked: "Did I say something about no trouble on this trip? When will I learn to keep my big mouth shut?"

CHAPTER II

Captain Turk Mallane

RICK paced the hotel lobby, walking back and forth in front of the couch where Scotty and Chahda sat. Now and then he went to the door and looked out, watching for Dr. Warren's station wagon.

"Relax," Scotty pleaded. "You'll wear a groove in the rug."

"They soon be here," Chahda added.

"I can't relax," Rick said worriedly. "How do we know what's going on? Those two men may be up to something serious."

"Well, acting like a caged tiger won't help," Scotty said reasonably. "Sit down."

The boys had returned to their cottage to find a note from Hartson Brant. The scientists had gone out with Dr. Warren and would return at seven for dinner.

Since then, Rick's always active imagination had expanded the conversation he had overheard into a definite warning of impending disaster. Had he known where the *Tarpon* was berthed, he would have hurried to the ship and conducted a personal search.

"If I've ever seen a hard character, it was that guy in the grey suit," he stated. "He's up to no good."

"Sure," Scotty soothed. "But don't fret about it. We'll take care of him."

A car spattered gravel in the driveway and Rick was out the door like a shot. In spite of their professed calmness, Scotty and Chahda were right behind him. Dr. Warren's station wagon was just pulling up to the door.

Rick saw that the car was full of men, but he paid no attention to them, hurrying to his father as soon as Hartson Brant got out of the front seat.

"Gosh, I'm glad you're back, Dad! Something . . ." he stopped, seeing strangers getting out.

"Gentlemen," Hartson Brant said, "I want you to meet the younger members of the party." He introduced the boys to three members of the Pacific Ethnographic Society. Then, as a fourth stranger followed Professor Gordon from the car, Rick's breath stopped. It was the man in the grey suit!

"Here's someone you want to meet, Rick," Gordon said. "Turk, this is Rick Brant. The two with him are Scotty and Chahda. Boys, meet Captain Turk Mallane, skipper of the *Tarpon*."

Rick heard Scotty and Chahda gasp, then start chuckling behind him. He swallowed his embarrassment and shook hands with the swarthy man in the grey suit. He looked into piercing black eyes.

Mallane asked cordially, "I've seen you boys before, haven't I?"

"This afternoon," Rick agreed. "We were at the hotel beach."

"I thought so," Mallane nodded. "Digger Sears brought me some supply reports. He's our mate. You'll meet him tomorrow. He told me that we are almost fully provisioned, barring a few fresh things and Diesel oil which arrives tomorrow. We can be on our way in a day or two, as far as the ship is concerned."

"We should be able to leave on Saturday," Hartson Brant said.

Professor Gordon led the way into the dining room. It was to be a semi-formal dinner, given by the members of the Pacific Ethnographic Society in honour of the Spindrift party. The boys fell behind the scientists and Rick faced Scotty's and Chahda's wide grins.

"Cheer up," Scotty jibed. "Jumping at conclusions is about the only exercise you get."

"The captain and the other mans talked only of supplies," Chahda said, grinning. "No bombs. Most too bad."

"Well," Rick said, "I'm glad you two weren't worried."

He was relieved to find that the two mysterious strangers hadn't been mysterious at all, but members of the expedition. Other Spindrift expeditions had run into unforeseen difficulties and he had become apprehensive about the slightest indications of trouble. Maybe he had been right after all. Maybe this expedition was going to be as peaceful as a Spindrift Island picnic.

At dinner, Rick was seated next to Turk Mallane. Across from them were Scotty and Chahda. The scientists, seated at the other end of the table, lost no time in getting into technical discussion of Pacific natives. Turk and the boys tried to listen, but were soon lost in a maze of such scientific matters as the cephalic index, language roots, Mongoloid folds, and so on.

"Is making my head ache," Chahda complained. "Such words!"

"I'm baffled, too," Scotty agreed.

"We'll get Professor Gordon to give us some background dope," Rick said. "His hobby is archaeology. He'll be the expert on this expedition."

"Good thing there's one expert," Turk Mallane said, smiling. "Gordon tells me we'll be searching for artifacts. I wouldn't know an artifact if it bit me."

"Neither would I," Rick agreed. He was beginning to like Turk Mallane in spite of his first impression. He asked: "Were you the skipper of the trawler when Professor Gordon chartered her?"

"No, I came later," Turk replied. "I was taking life easy and wasn't particularly anxious to get back to work. Then I saw Gordon's ad in the Honolulu *Star Bulletin*. He wanted a qualified master mariner who knew the western Pacific, and one with experience in handling diving equipment. Well, that business about the diving equipment got me interested. I used to be a salvage diver, and before the war I was master of a salvage tug. I answered the ad and met Gordon and he told me something about this machine you call the Submobile. Before I knew it, I was all excited about the expedition and getting a crew together."

"Is the crew very big?" Scotty inquired.

"No. Just Digger Sears, three seamen, and a cook."

"That doesn't seem like enough men to run such a big boat," Rick said. "Won't you have to work pretty hard?"

"We'll stand short watches, four hours on and four off," Turk explained. "We've done it before, and I'm interested enough in the expedition to want to cut corners and save a little money."

"Salvage diving must be exciting," Scotty remarked.

"Like anything else. Sometimes it is, at other times it's just a dull grind." Turk smiled at the three eager faces around him. "Have you lads any idea what you're getting into? Far as I can see, all hands are pretty casual about going down 600 or 700 feet, but it's something to marvel at, I tell you! Do you know the formula for figuring water pressure?"

"It says in Alm-in-ack," Chahda said, "one atmosphere pressure for each thirty-three feet depth."

"Right. And one atmosphere is 14.7 pounds per square inch. That's a lot of pressure. It's what kills divers, and it's what has kept men from salvaging ships in water deeper than 300 feet. And here you are, calm as clams about going down twice that far."

"But mens are going deeper than 300 feets," Chahda objected. "Record is 525 feet. Also divers once find ship at 400 feet. Then is scientists going away deep, like Sahib Dr. Beebe and Sahib Professor Picard."

Turk Mallane looked at Chahda with surprised admiration. "You have the facts right at your finger tips, all right!"

"He reads *The World Almanac*," Rick explained. "He has more facts in his head than the sea has fish."

"Well, let's examine his facts," Turk said companionably. "It's true that a diver once went to 525 feet. He was in an armoured shell, and he went down in a lake in Bavaria. And divers in similar armoured shells found the treasure ship *Egypt* at 400 feet. But these armoured shells were practically useless. The divers had to depend on mechanical arms for their salvage work, and the water pressure was so great it locked the arms. No, you can discount the armoured suits. The only practical salvage work up to now has been done in flexible suits such as Navy divers wear, and the record dive in one of those is only a little more than 300 feet."

"I'd hate to tear my pants at that depth," Scotty said.

"And with good reason," Turk agreed. "A tear in your suit at that depth would let the air escape and the sea would push in on you with a force of over 140 tons! Yes, that's the figure. Take 2,100 square inches for the area of the human body and apply the formula."

"The Submobile is stressed for even greater pressures than that," Rick put in.

"So Gordon told me," Turk nodded. "I merely mentioned the pressure figures to show you what a great thing it will be if this trip proves that salvage is possible down to 100 fathoms, or even more."

Turk Mallane *had* put the venture in a new light. Rick had known about ocean pressures and pressure formulas, but not until the captain put them in terms of a diver in a flexible suit had he appreciated what pressure really meant.

"Suppose we can prove that salvage is possible, even at 100 fathoms," Turk continued. "Can you picture what you'll have started?"

"Not understanding," Chahda murmured apologetically.

"The greatest treasure hunt in the world!" Turk pointed out. "Think, lads. There are hundreds—no, thousands—of ships lying just below a diver's reach." He pointed a finger at Chahda. "Check your *World Almanac* on that. See the list in the *Almanac* of ships sunk in the last hundred years. And that's only a part of them. There are galleons loaded with plate and bullion and pieces of eight and cross money and doubloons— ancient wealth to make your head spin!"

Turk's voice had lifted in volume until all the scientists were listening. Rick looked at the captain and saw a strange glint in his black eyes. It was odd about Turk's eyes. They were usually as expressionless as two marbles. Even when he laughed, the mirth never reached his eyes.

Rick remarked on the fact later, as the boys climbed into their beds.

"I noticed his eyes, too," Scotty said thoughtfully. "Turk's a hard customer, but I suppose salvage diving is no business for softies. I can't decide whether I like him or not."

"Same here," Rick agreed. He cautioned, "Keep your voices down. He might be taking a walk or something." They had learned that Turk was staying at the hotel until sailing time. He had the cottage diagonally across the path from them.

Chahda spoke up. "What I think, Captain Turk tries hard to make us like him. That is why he is being nice tonight."

The Hindu boy had put into words something that Rick had sensed during dinner—that Turk was going out of his way to be affable. "That's nothing against him," he pointed out. "In fact, it's in his favour. If he wants to be friends, we'll meet him more than halfway."

"Sure," Scotty agreed. "Only I think I'll wait until we've been at sea for a few days before I decide whether we'll ever be real buddies. There's nothing like rough weather to tell you what a guy is really like."

And on that note they went to sleep.

CHAPTER III

The Man with the Broken Nose

PROFESSOR GORDON banged the screen door loudly and shouted, "Hit the deck! Rise and shine! It's a new day."

Startled to rude wakefulness, Rick sat up and blinked in the sunlight that streamed through the windows. "What is it?"

"Roll out," Gordon ordered cheerfully. "There's just time for a quick swim and breakfast before we go to the docks."

Scotty and Chahda sat up, their sleepiness gone at the reminder that today would see the entire party united with their equipment.

In a moment they were out of their pyjamas and into bathing trunks, racing for the water front. As they passed Turk Mallane's cottage, the captain called a greeting.

Rick went headlong into the water and headed out into the sea with a powerful crawl stroke. He felt like a million this morning. In a little while they would meet Hobart Zircon, take the equipment from the *Aloha*, and start getting it ready for the trip to Kwangara. Today they would have a chance to see the *Tarpon*, too, and get acquainted with their new home.

Refreshed and fully awake after their swim, the boys hurried back to their cottage, showered, and dressed. Then they joined the scientists at breakfast. Turk Mallane had already eaten and was on his way to the trawler.

Breakfast was hurried, because the SS *Aloha* was due to dock early. Professor Gordon had already made arrangements with the port officials for immediate unloading and had ordered a trailer truck to transport the equipment.

By the time Dr. Warren had picked them up in his station wagon and taken them to the dock, the great white bulk of the steamship was in sight and tugs were warping her into the berth.

The scientists and the boys watched as the gangway was lowered and passengers started coming off. A band had materialized and was giving out lustily with *Aloha Oe*. Flower women, almost hidden under fragrant flower leis, were everywhere.

Rick watched for Professor Hobart Zircon and saw him come down the gangway.

The big scientist's voice rose above the noise. "Well! A most imposing reception committee! Greetings, my friends."

Everything about Professor Zircon was big, from his voice to his massive frame. He radiated energy and good spirits as he shook hands all around, greeting Rick, Scotty, and Chahda with the warmth of an old trail comrade. Then he got right down to business.

"Everything is arranged. We can unload at once, if the port officials are agreeable. You've seen them? And how about a truck?"

"All arranged," Hartson Brant told him. "Suppose you and I go aboard, Hobart? I'll stand by the winch

operator while you take charge in the hold. Gordon will
see that the load is distributed properly on the truck.
Rick and Scotty can help him. Chahda, take Professor
Zircon's baggage checks, please, and see that his personal
luggage is put aboard the truck."

"Is there something I can do?" Dr. Warren asked.

"Yes, Paul. Would you take these duplicate manifests
and check off the crates as they are loaded on the truck?"
Hartson Brant handed Dr. Warren the lists.

"Did you see the truck outside?" Gordon asked Rick.
"Yes? Then direct the driver, if you will. We'll want the
trailer platform right under the forward deck and parallel
with the edge of the dock."

The platform trailer looked big enough to carry a
house, but the Hawaiian driver swung it into place
with effortless skill as Rick directed him. On the deck
of the *Aloha*, the cargo hatch was already off and the
winch operator was standing by, Hartson Brant at his
side.

Almost at once the big wooden crates began to arrive,
swinging down from the deck in cargo nets. Rick, Scotty,
and Professor Gordon pushed them into place on the forward end of the platform. There was a short breathing
spell, then four smaller boxes arrived. Rick saw by their
markings that they contained personal equipment and
stuff for camping. The cargo net arrived with three round
objects wrapped in heavy burlap. Rick identified those as
cables, one for the salvage arms of the Submobile, the
other for electric power.

"That's all," Dr. Warren announced, consulting his
lists. "Now for the Submobile."

Rick watched, his head tilted back until his neck
creaked. Up on deck, the winch turned slowly, the

creaking of the metal blocks showing an increased strain on it. Little by little a silvery mound like the back of a small whale came into sight. The Submobile was lifted clear of the deck and dangled in mid-air.

The Submobile was imposing. It had the shape of a small dirigible, ten feet long and six feet at its greatest diameter. Steel plates concealed and protected the fused-quartz observation ports and the places where the Sonoscope, the extension arms, the propellers and other equipment would be attached to the blunt nose. It was bolted into a steel framework cradle that gave it a solid resting place when it sat on deck or on the sea bottom.

The winch operator swung the Submobile over the side and began to lower it by inches while Professor Gordon ran anxiously from one place to another, sighting to see if it would land properly. Rick noticed that a crowd had gathered. He heard the buzz of speculation.

"Midget submarine," one man suggested.

"Naw. It's a new kind of buoy."

Rick saw that the Submobile was going to land just right. He marvelled at the skill of the winch operator and moved back against the wall for a clearer view of the ship's deck.

The Submobile descended an inch at a time and settled into place with feather lightness. Rick started to wave at his father, but a commotion a few feet away distracted him. He turned to see what all the noise was about.

A dock worker, who held a big packing case, was arguing with a Japanese standing in a doorway.

"Come out o' there," the dock worker shouted. "Blast it, can't you read? 'No Loitering in This Doorway.' Now come out. This is a busy spot, and I got to get inside before I drop this thing."

The Japanese started to move away, then he saw Rick and hastily drew back. The angry dock worker put down the case he held, reached in with a brawny arm and pulled. The Japanese came out of the doorway like a cork out of a bottle. He cast a swift look at Rick, then scuttled out through the gateway.

Rick watched him, puzzled. He walked up to the dock worker. "What was he doing?"

"The Jap? Just standin' in the way. He was blockin' traffic."

"Funny he didn't want to move," Rick said.

"Yeah. Looked like he wanted to hide. Queer jokers, these Japs. Never know what they'll do." The dock worker picked up his case and carried it into the warehouse as Rick held the door for him.

From what had the Jap been hiding? Or from whom? Rick had the uncomfortable feeling that he had been the one from whom the Japanese hid. He remembered how the fellow had ducked back into the doorway at sight of him. Why should he act like that? There was nothing wrong with watching the Submobile. Plenty of others were doing it.

But he was sure of one thing: He wouldn't forget the man's face. At some time in the past a sharp edge, perhaps of a Samurai sword, had struck the Jap's nose on the bridge, breaking it and leaving a bluish scar.

The others were already at work lashing the load of crates to the trailer. Heavy ropes were passed over the Submobile, through the steel lift ring at the top, then under the trailer platform. Its own weight would keep it in place, but the Spindrift scientists had learned to take extra precautions.

Hartson Brant called, "Who'll volunteer to ride with the load?"

"We will," Rick said hastily. "Scotty and Chahda and I."

"All right. We'll meet you at the ship. Have your driver follow Dr. Warren's car."

Rick gave the driver instructions, then climbed up on the crates with Scotty and Chahda. The trailer rolled out through the pier gate and into the street.

"Why the frown?" Scotty asked.

Rick told him of the Japanese who had acted so strangely.

"A Nip, huh?" Scotty said. "Do you suppose his actions had anything to do with the equipment?"

"I don't know," Rick answered. "His being in the doorway might have been a coincidence. Only why did he duck back when he saw me?"

"You frighten him, maybe," Chahda said. "Could happen. When I first see famous Brant face, I am frighten too."

"That's enough out of you, Gunga Din," Rick retorted. "But seriously, we'd better keep our eyes open."

"We can't afford to take chances," Scotty agreed.

The big trailer moved through traffic, the object of much attention from pedestrians.

"They like its looks," Scotty said, winking at Rick. "Too bad we can't leave it shiny."

Chahda took the bait. "We painting it?"

"Yep. Bright red."

"But why is painting red?"

"Because of the big fish we might run into," Scotty explained seriously. "If we left it shiny silver, some big fish might mistake it for a can of sardines."

B

Chahda nodded gravely. "Is most true. But painting red is also mistake. Maybe along comes big fish and thinks it is a radish."

Rick laughed. "He's too sharp for you, Scotty."

"Sharp like tick," Chahda agreed, chuckling.

"Tack," Scotty corrected. "I'll blunt his sharp edge one of these days."

The trailer truck followed Dr. Warren's station wagon across the bridge over the Ala Wai Canal, turned right, and came to a stop next to a row of piers. The boys jumped down, and Rick looked around eagerly for his first glimpse of the ship that was to be their home.

"There she is," he exclaimed, pointing at the distinctive lines of the trawler.

Turk Mallane appeared in the doorway of the pilot-house and waved. "Come aboard," he called.

The boys accepted the invitation with alacrity. Turk shook hands all around, then introduced them to the thin, bald man who had been with him in the pavilion. "This is Digger Sears, boys, mate of the *Tarpon* for this cruise. He'll show you around."

"Three husky blokes to make seamen out of," Digger said jovially. "Let's hop to it, lads. I'm thinkin' you'll be wantin' to see what kind o' dinkum tub you've shipped aboard of."

The *Tarpon* was a typical trawler, the superstructure set forward leaving considerable deck space aft. On that open space, where huge nets with tons of fish had once been dumped, the Submobile would rest. The heavy booms that had been designed to take the weight of a loaded net would serve to handle the Submobile, which was surprisingly light for its size, due to special light-weight alloys used in its construction.

Below decks, in what had once been fish holds, cabins had been built. In one space forward, a big Army-type refrigerator had been installed. Rick opened the door and went inside, shivering in the sudden low temperature. The refrigerator room was jammed with food. Meat hung on hooks up by the freezing pipes, and down lower crates of fresh vegetables rested. There were crates of oranges, too, and an open barrel of apples near the door.

"Only a few feet from the cabins," Scotty said with satisfaction. "Handy for a late snack."

Rick's retort was stilled by the sudden appearance of a smiling black face.

"This is Otera," Digger Sears said. "Only a bush boy from down Hebrides way, but a dinkum cook for all that. Otera, say a cheery word to the lads."

Otera had bushy, frizzy hair that stood straight up like a starched mop, and a smile that seemed to light up the hold. "Dis fella marster want kai-kai?" he inquired hopefully.

"That's *bêché-de-mer*," Scotty explained. "Pidgin English, most people call it. It's a real language instead of just bad English. He wants to know if we three want anything to eat."

Digger Sears looked at Scotty, his long face thoughtful. "You been in the Islands?" he asked.

"The Marines," Scotty said briefly.

"Aye? A fightin' lot, them Yank Marines. 'Most as good as the Aussie Ninth."

Rick had heard of the famous Australian Ninth Division. "Were you in the Ninth?" he asked. "I should think you would have been in the Navy."

"Not 'arf!" Digger exclaimed. "I figgered I'd end up

on a Limey ship for sure, and I don't like Limeys. I'm an Aussie, I am. No Limey nyvy for this bloke."

Rick grinned, more at Digger's accent than at his explanation.

"What is up there?" Chahda asked, pointing forward.

"Paint locker and a glory hole with odds and ends o' junk." Digger pronounced it "pynt."

Up on deck, the boys were introduced to the three seamen. They looked and dressed alike, in worn dungarees and soiled shirts. They were dark of skin, and rather sullen. Scotty christened them "Dewey, Hughey, and Lewey" after Donald Duck's three nephews, because, as he explained, "They look alike and act alike, and they're sailors."

"Besides," Rick added, "we could never remember those names."

The three seamen, Gordon explained later, were part Hawaiian, part Portuguese, and part something else he hadn't figured out as yet. Their names were Hawaiian and seemed to consist mostly of vowels and the letter K.

The boys went ashore, to find the trailer already being unloaded with the aid of the boatyard operator who had brought his ship crane into service. The crates were being stacked around the walls of a vacant boathouse directly behind the *Tarpon*.

"What are we going to do with the Submobile?" Rick asked his father.

"Stand it next to the boathouse door. The weather can't hurt it, and we'll need the room in the boathouse for unpacking."

Scotty asked: "How about guards?"

"I've arranged that with Mallane. The crew will stand watches until we sail. It won't be hard on them. They'll just look out at the stuff once in a while."

Rick was satisfied. The boatyard was a pretty public place, and the equipment was within fifty feet of the trawler. It would be safe.

The Submobile was the last to be unloaded. The crane, designed to lift good-sized boats completely out of the water, lifted the undersea craft with ease and placed it against the boathouse wall.

After a quick lunch, prepared by the smiling Otera, Hartson Brant consulted his watch. "It's still early. We could uncrate our personal equipment and stow it aboard. That would leave only the big stuff to uncrate tomorrow."

"A good idea," Gordon agreed.

All hands turned to and dragged the smaller crates to the centre of the boathouse floor. Rick and Scotty found tools and began ripping open the wooden crates while Gordon showed the others which cabins had been assigned to them.

Chahda returned and reported that the boys had been given the forward cabin, right next to the refrigeration room. "Rick is aviator," the Hindu boy said, referring to the fact that Rick was a licensed pilot. "He should get high bed, maybe?"

"You mean the upper bunk? We'll toss for it." Rick took a coin from his pocket while Scotty and Chahda followed suit. "Odd man get the upper bunk," Rick said.

They flipped, and Scotty's coin came down tails while the other two showed heads.

"Okay," Scotty said. "I'll do the high flying on this cruise. Now, let's get our own stuff out of the crates and take it aboard."

The boys had been allotted one locker box apiece

for their clothing. Each found his own, removed it from the wooden shipping crate, and carried it to the cabin on the trawler.

Scotty sniffed. "I know what Dr. Warren meant. This place smells like a fish market."

"I noticed it," Rick agreed, "but it's not bad. The paint smell covers most of it."

Suddenly Chahda held up his hand for silence. "What is noise?"

Rick heard a scuffling from somewhere overhead, then a yell of pain. Instantly he was on his way to the deck ladder, Scotty and Chahda on his heels.

"It's forward," Scotty said.

Pots and pans fell with a terrific crash. Rick sprinted for the galley, found the door and looked in.

Otera, the cook, was on the floor in a litter of cooking utensils. He was holding his head in both hands, and cringing away from Digger Sears, who was standing over him.

"Blasted black scum!" Digger roared. "Give me any of yer lip and I'll knock yer black head clean off, blimey if I won't!"

"What's going on?" Rick demanded.

Otera started to get to his feet, but Digger's fist knocked him to the floor again. The cook subsided, whimpering.

"Stop that," Rick said angrily. "What are you hitting him for?"

"I'll teach the blighter a lesson," Digger growled. "Give me any of his bloomin' back talk and I'll carve his tongue out."

Hartson Brant demanded from the doorway, "What's happening here?"

Digger's face changed at the sight of the scientist. "The filthy bloke never washes his pots. I took 'im up on it and he gave me some back chat."

"Is that any reason for striking him?" Hartson Brant asked coldly.

"It's the only language these blasted gooks know," Digger said sullenly.

"You'll keep your hands off him, and off everyone else on this ship," Hartson Brant snapped.

Digger's pale eyes flamed. "You ain't the captain," he retorted.

"I'm the leader of the expedition," Hartson Brant stated, "and I'm responsible for all aboard. You'll take orders from me, Sears, as well as from Captain Mallane. And if you don't like that idea, pack your duffel and get out. We can find another mate."

For a moment Digger's eyes locked with the scientist's, then he looked away. "Aye aye," he said, and pushed out of the galley.

Hartson Brant looked at the boys. "Where is Captain Mallane?"

"I think he went ashore, sir," Scotty said. "He was telling Professor Gordon something about checking up on the delivery of Diesel oil."

"All right. I'll have a talk with him when he gets back." Hartson Brant turned and went aft.

Rick helped Otera to his feet. The native cook managed a feeble grin, rubbing a prominent bruise on his forehead.

"It won't happen again," Rick told him kindly. "You don't have to be afraid of the mate any more."

Otera brightened. He looked at Scotty and Chahda, and his smile flashed. He bobbed his head gratefully.

"Dis fella young marster, he get plenty good kai-kai. My word!"

The boys left him alone to straighten up his galley and walked toward the stern of the ship.

"He's our friend," Scotty said. "He said he'd see that we were well fed."

"What's that 'my word' stuff?" Rick asked.

"It's his way of being emphatic," Scotty explained. "Sort of a verbal exclamation point."

The scientists had stowed their personal stuff and were uncrating the cases of camping equipment. There were two pyramid tents, complete with metal tent stakes, cots, pads, mosquito netting, and a small, electric lighting system. The scientists hoped to find a suitable place for a base camp, since there would not be enough room on the ship for cleaning and examining the large bits of the temple they hoped to find.

In a short time the camping equipment was stowed in a spare gear room aboard ship, and Hartson Brant announced that it was time to return to the hotel for dinner.

"Mallane hasn't returned," he said. "However, tomorrow will be soon enough to talk with him. I don't intend to stand for any brutality on this expedition!"

Zircon, Gordon, and the boys nodded silent agreement.

Rick debated telling his father about the Japanese he had seen at the dock and decided not to. Hartson Brant was upset over the incident aboard ship. There was no point in giving him something else to worry about unless the Jap's actions proved to have some bearing on the expedition.

CHAPTER IV

Caught by Infrared

RICK was feeling restless, and he couldn't account for it. Everything was going smoothly, the equipment was well guarded, nothing remained to be done but the uncrating and stowing of the heavy Submobile gear and electronic equipment. They would sail on Saturday.

Perhaps his uneasiness grew out of the fact that everything was progressing too well. There had never before been a Spindrift experiment or expedition without something unforeseen cropping up. The very nature of the scientific projects seemed to invite the unexpected.

The incident at the dock stuck in his mind, too. He had tried to think up reasons for the Jap's strange actions, but none came to mind. That in itself was disturbing, because he had learned that there was a reason behind every event and he was afraid that the Jap's reason for hiding was somehow connected with the expedition.

Scotty came up to where Rick sat on the cottage steps.

"Let's take a walk," Scotty invited. "It's a nice night."

"All right. Where's Chahda?"

"He's in with the professors. They're talking about archaeology. It's away over my head."

They walked down the path toward the water front, noticing that most of the cottages were dark.

"I guess people don't stay home nights," Scotty said. "It's too early for anyone to be in bed."

Rick looked toward Turk Mallane's cottage. "The skipper is out, too. Decided whether you like him or not?"

"I'm reserving judgment," Scotty said. "Ask me in a week."

The hotel water front was dark, the pavilion a black bulk against the faintly phosphorescent water. But out on the reef there were flickering lights. Rick watched them for a moment.

"Wonder what those are?"

"Torches," Scotty told him. "Hawaiians fishing by torchlight. They'll be moving in toward shore in a while and you can see them."

"What are they catching?"

"Search me. Squid, maybe, and small fish of some kind."

It was a colourful sight. Now and then, out beyond the reef, Rick saw the lights of a vessel.

"We ought to have a picture of it," he said idly.

Scotty took him up on it. "Why not? We have the camera, and we could get some good shots with infra-red."

"You're the eager beaver," Rick said. "You get the camera."

"Just to show you my heart's in the right place, I'll do it." Scotty trotted back up the path toward the cottage. He returned presently accompanied by Chahda.

Scotty was carrying the speed graphic. He had attached the flash gun and inserted an infrared film pack. Extra bulbs were in his pocket.

"I brought company," he greeted Rick. "Chahda wanted to see the torch fishermen."

The Hindu boy watched the moving torches for a while, then he asked, "But how they catching fishes with torches?"

Scotty took the infrared bulb out of the flash gun and reinserted it more firmly. Rick grinned. He knew that Scotty was thinking up some fantastic yarn.

"It's the heat," Scotty said at last.

"Heat? How you catch fishes with heat?"

"I'm surprised at you," Scotty said gravely. "You should be able to figure that out. Look, the torches are hot, right? Well, the fishermen hold them close to the water. And what happens? The water gets warm. The fish get warm, too. Now do you see?"

Chahda thought it over. "Not see yet. Try some more."

"Okay. What happens when you get warm? You have to sweat, don't you? Well, how can you sweat under water? You can't. So the fish come to the surface to sweat and the fishermen hit 'em over the head with clubs."

"Very good system," Chahda said soberly. "But more better if they use onions, I think, like in India."

Rick waited, smiling in the darkness. Chahda had fallen for Scotty's tall yarn, and had put out bait of his own. Scotty knew the bit about onions was bait, too, but he wouldn't be able to suppress his lively curiosity long.

Sure enough, after a long silence, Scotty asked: "How do they use onions? For bait?"

"Kind of bait," Chahda agreed. "They put peeled onion on string and lower into water. Makes poor fishes' eyes watering. Poor fishes coming to top to cry—bop! Gets hit with club also. You see?"

"I see," Scotty said with a chuckle.

Rick noticed that the torches were coming nearer. "Think we could get a shot now?" he asked.

"We can try," Scotty said. "Here. You're the camera expert."

Rick took the speed graphic and shot a picture of the nearest torch. With luck, the developed film would show the fisherman as well. Infrared could see things the eye couldn't.

It was late when the fishermen finally moved out of sight. Rick rose and stretched. He set the camera for one more picture, intending to take a shot of the open sea, thinking that he might get an interesting view of the surf on the reef. Then he decided against wasting the film.

"Want to turn in?" he asked his friends. "We'll have a lot to do tomorrow."

"It's all right with me," Scotty agreed.

"Also," Chahda said.

They walked up the path through almost total darkness. Then, as they neared their cottage, Scotty suddenly stopped.

"Someone's in the shrubbery to our left," he whispered in Rick's ear.

Rick tensed, listening, but his ears weren't jungle-trained, as Scotty's were.

Chahda quietly had moved close to the shrubs. Suddenly he jumped into them, giving a wild yell.

There was instant response. A man hurtled out to

the path, fell, but was up on his feet and running before Rick or Scotty could grab him. Instinctively Rick brought his camera up and clicked the flash button just as he saw the blur of a white face.

"After him," Scotty called.

Chahda was already sprinting up the path after the intruder. Rick ran to the cottage steps, put the camera down, and joined in the chase. He had no doubts about chasing the man, whoever he was. If he turned out to be a guest, he would have some explanation. If he wasn't a guest, there must have been some illegal reason for hiding in the shrubbery.

The fleeing intruder crashed through a hedge, ducked between two cottages, and ran down another path. Rick and Scotty hit the hedge at the same time, and somehow got in each other's way. They crashed to the soft turf.

"Here!" Chahda called. He had cut around another cottage and was still after the intruder. Rick and Scotty got to their feet and raced after him.

Rick saw that they were running back toward the water front. Then he heard Chahda's voice again, to the right. The man must be running along the sea wall!

The chase ended abruptly at a high board fence. Chahda was running along the fence, looking for some sign of the quarry. In a moment he called, "I think he go over."

"Up you go," Scotty said. He held out his cupped hands. Rick put his foot in them and jumped, coming to rest on top of the fence. He looked down into what was evidently a big lumberyard with piles of drying wood. There were a dozen exits the intruder might have taken. They would never catch him now.

"Coming down," he called, and dropped lightly to the ground beside Scotty and Chahda. He explained what he had seen.

"I wonder what he was up to," Scotty mused. "Something queer, because he wouldn't have run otherwise."

"I thinking maybe I jump into bush and scare him out, then you catch," Chahda explained.

"He moved too fast," Rick said ruefully. "He caught us flat-footed."

"Did you get a picture?" Scotty asked. "I saw the bulb go off."

"It ought to be a good one," Rick told him, starting back to the cottage. "I shot just as he looked back. Let's develop it and see."

"The developing stuff is on the *Tarpon*," Scotty reminded him.

"Sure. But it's not very late."

Rick put the camera away, first tucking the exposed film pack in his pocket. Then they hiked to the boatyard, finding it ablaze with lights.

Otera was sitting on the afterdeck, smoking a stub of a pipe.

"We have something we want to do," Rick told him. "Where are the others?"

Otera shook his head. "No savee. Me one fella watch-boy. Good fella too much!" He grinned widely.

"He doesn't know where the others are. He's on watch," Scotty translated. "Do you know where the developing kit is?"

"Yes," Rick said. "I put it away myself."

He led the way below decks and took the compact developing kit from the storage room. There was running water in the bathroom, and room to lay out the trays. Rick filled them from the bottles of prepared fluid, then switched out the light and went to work.

"Let's have the light," he said presently. He took the film out of the water bath and waved it back and forth, shaking off the excess liquid. Then he held it to the light.

He had caught the running figure from the waist up, and the face, looking back over the shoulder, was plain. A queer sensation travelled down his spine. Clearly visible, even in the negative film, was a sharp break in the bridge of the man's nose, and the eyes had a slant look under stiff black hair.

"The Jap!" Rick exclaimed. "The same one I saw at the pier this afternoon!"

CHAPTER V

The Warning

To THE amazement of Hartson Brant when he came out of his cottage at seven in the morning, the three younger members of the expedition were already up. Led by Rick, they were sniffing around in the shrubbery like three eager beagles.

The scientist walked over to where the boys hunted. "Looking for edible roots or fruits?" he asked dryly. "I can't imagine anything but food that would get you three up at this time in the morning without prompting."

Rick looked up from his examination of the soft turf. "Hello, Dad. We're looking for . . . gosh, I don't know what we're looking for. A clue, I guess."

The scientists had been asleep when the boys returned from the trawler, and Rick had decided not to disturb them. Now, he told his father the whole story, beginning with his first sight of the Japanese with the broken nose on the dock. He concluded, "He was hiding in the shrubbery next to Turk Mallane's cottage."

Hartson Brant studied the film negative thoughtfully, then handed it to Hobart Zircon, who had just come out of the cottage. He outlined Rick's story briefly. "What do you think, Hobart?"

The big scientist examined the negative. "I don't know what to think," he boomed. "You don't believe it's just a coincidence, Rick?"

"It could be," Rick admitted, "but you've often said yourself that you don't believe in that kind of coincidence."

"Maybe Turk Mallane knows something about the Jap," Scotty suggested. "He was hiding near Turk's cottage."

"I'm blessed if I can think of any reason why this Japanese should be interested in us," Hartson Brant said. "Suppose we have breakfast. We can ask Captain Mallane for his opinion later."

Professor Gordon joined them as they walked toward the dining room, and Rick had to tell the story once more. Gordon, like the others, had nothing to suggest.

It wasn't until they had reached the trawler that they had a chance to talk with Turk. The broad-shouldered captain listened to Rick's story, then took the film and looked at it.

"Never saw the man before," he said finally. "I'm sure I don't know what he was doing near my cottage. Couldn't it have been your cottages that interested him? They're close together."

Rick shrugged. Anything was possible, since they had no evidence either way. He watched Turk examine the negative again before handing it back, and somehow he got the impression that the captain wasn't being entirely frank. He was too casual about the whole business.

Hartson Brant called the Spindrift group together. "Turk Mallane informs me that he can get clearances today, so we can sail in the morning. The Diesel oil was delivered right after we left last night, and all ship's supplies and food are aboard. Our own personal gear is aboard, with the camping supplies. If we pitch in, the equipment can be aboard by nightfall."

He assigned them to various tasks. Rick and Scotty were to uncrate the equipment and Chahda was to check off each piece against a master list. Rick got further instructions on the proper order in which to open the cases to make stowage simpler; then he and Scotty went to work.

The salvage apparatus for the Submobile was first. They uncrated what looked like a small steam shovel with powerful jaws. It operated on the same principle, and had been designed for picking up small objects from the ocean floor. It had no name other than "the scoop." In the same crate were two extension arms that operated on the scissors principle. Each was equipped with a powerful ring snap that would hold the steel salvage cable.

Other cases contained the brass ball from which the Sonoscope impulses would be transmitted, electric motors, three bronze propellers, a host of electronic equipment, oxygen cylinders, chemicals, and specially prepared explosive charges.

Rick found one case without markings and called Chahda. The Hindu boy consulted his list, checking case numbers against the diminishing pile of crates.

"Not here," he reported.

Rick looked the odd case over. It was much smaller than the others, and not very heavy. He called the scientists, who were storing the Submobile equipment in accessible places on the ship.

"An extra case?" Hartson Brant said. "That's odd."

Professor Gordon came out of the hold in time to hear the remark. "What extra case? Oh, that's probably mine." He went to the boathouse with Rick and looked at it. "Yes. That's mine. A few necessities I collected in Honolulu. I had them put in a wooden box and left them here to be taken aboard and stowed with the rest."

"That's a relief," Rick said. "For a minute I thought maybe that Jap had planted a bomb or something." He ripped open the case and Gordon began enumerating the items as they were taken out.

"This stuff is for keeping us healthy," he said. "I tried to think of everything. First of all, an ultraviolet sterilizer lamp. That's for treatment of any fungus infections we pick up, and also for sterilizing any native fruits or vegetables we might find."

"Good idea," Scotty said approvingly.

Gordon took out a large, pack-type spray gun. It had a cylindrical tank with a harness to carry it on one's back, a pump for building up air pressure, and a hose with a trigger release.

"This is for DDT. If the mosquitoes are bad, we can spray the area and perhaps cut down the population of malaria carriers. The DDT is in those cans. I got the powder rather than liquid, since it's cleaner to use. The spray will handle it."

Scotty nodded approval. "I should have thought of those things myself," he said.

Rick picked out two smaller cans. "What are these?"

"Fluoride powder," Gordon told him. "That's to prevent tooth trouble, which is prevalent in the islands. I got together with a biochemist friend of Dr. Warren's and we worked out the formula for mixing the fluoride with regular tooth powder. You'll also find a spare first-aid kit in there."

Rick grinned. "We could practically stock a hospital. Not to mention a bug extermination plant."

"It's not funny," Scotty said. "I spent a long time in Navy hospitals with malaria because we didn't have enough insecticide to keep the mosquito population down."

"And I," Gordon added, "once spent six weeks in bed because there were no treatment lamps to check the spread of a fungus infection I picked up. I also might add that I now have four less teeth."

Rick apologized, and helped carry the equipment aboard, stowing it with the camping gear. Professor Zircon brought Scotty's rifle, which had been packed with some of the electronic equipment. "You'll want this in your cabin," he boomed. "Might get a shot at a cannibal or two, eh?"

"Could be." Scotty grinned.

He took the rifle, which was protected by a plastic cover, down to the cabin. Rick followed, intending to start unpacking his locker box.

Chahda had had the same idea. His locker box was open, and the Hindu boy was crawling behind it, reaching under the bunk.

"Lose something?" Rick asked.

"Piece paper," Chahda called. "It blow from bunk."

There were no portholes in the below-decks cabins, but a ventilator blew in a constant stream of fresh air.

"Got it," Chahda said. He stood up, holding a scrap of brown paper. "I unpacking, and I see this blow by." He frowned suddenly, his eyes on the paper. "What is this?"

Rick took it and turned it over, examining it. It was an irregular scrap of ordinary wrapping paper. On one side were two words, crudely printed in pencil.

WACHOUT ASAMO

Rick handed the scrap of paper to Scotty. "Look at this."

"Doesn't make any sense," Scotty said after looking it over.

"Asamo," Rick said thoughtfully. "Doesn't that sound Japanese?"

"Maybe," Chahda agreed. "But what is 'wachout'?"

"Watch out," Scotty said. "Spelled wrong."

Rick agreed. "I think you're right. It should be: Watch out Asamo. But what is it? A warning?" He remembered the Japanese with the broken nose. Could his name have been Asamo?

"Could be," Scotty said. "But what if this is only a scrap torn from something else? Let's not go off half cocked. We'd get everyone excited about nothing."

That made sense to Rick. "We're up in the air over that business at the hotel last night," he said. "This is probably just a scrap of paper that happened to have a couple of words on it."

"Maybe," Chahda said doubtfully.

"I wouldn't mention it to the others," Scotty said. "But just in case something is up, let's be extra watchful. And I think it might be a good idea if we searched the ship before sailing. What do you say?"

"I'd thought of that," Rick agreed. "We could do it without anyone noticing. Just sort of prowl around until we had covered everything."

Digger Sears called from outside the cabin door. "You blokes in there? All hands needed on deck. We're bringing the Submobile aboard."

The boys hurried out and found the mate in the passageway. "Topside," Digger growled. "Ye're needed on the lines."

On the shore, the ship crane had been moved into position and its cable hooked through the lift ring of the Submobile—a circle of steel like an enormous doughnut, firmly welded to the top of the undersea craft. Heavy ropes had been attached to the cradle to aid in hauling it into position. Professor Gordon had consulted with Turk Mallane on the proper position and chalk marks had been sketched on the open afterdeck.

At a signal, the crane operator lifted the Submobile into the air and moved it to the ship. The Spindrift party and the crew took the trailing ropes and, directed by Hartson Brant, swung the Submobile into line with the chalk marks. At a signal the operator dropped the unwieldy thing to the deck, only an inch or two out of position. It was slid onto the marks by main strength, then bolted down with heavy screws an inch in diameter.

Rick looked at it with satisfaction. Nothing would budge the Submobile now unless the whole ship broke up.

By suppertime, everything was in place aboard, the boathouse was cleaned up, and everything was shipshape. Turk Mallane returned from Honolulu with a clean bill of health and clearance papers for the ship.

"We're set," Turk stated. "Name your own hour for leaving."

"Ten o'clock," Hartson Brant told him. "That will give us ample time for a good breakfast. Now, captain, about guards. Will you arrange for two men to stand by tonight?"

Turk looked at him keenly. "Afraid of trouble?"

"Not necessarily," Hartson Brant returned. "But we've learned not to take chances."

Rick thought that Turk seemed amused. However, the captain agreed readily enough.

"Tell you what," he said, "I'll check out of the hotel tonight and move aboard. Digger and I will take turns standing watch alongside the regular crew watch."

"That would be very good of you," Zircon boomed.

"If you still think there's something to watch out for," Turk continued, "we'll have a look at the ship in the morning just before we sail. Then your minds can be at rest."

"A good idea," Professor Gordon agreed. "I doubt that these precautions are necessary, but why take chances? It's just as easy to be on guard."

Turk Mallane turned to Rick. "Get a good night's sleep," he said jovially. "It's the high seas for us to-morrow!"

As they walked to the hotel, Scotty grinned at Rick. "Regular pals, you and Turk."

"I don't like it," Rick said shortly. There was something false about the captain's heartiness. But perhaps that was just his way. "What do you think about him suggesting that we search the ship?" he asked. "Funny he should have said that."

"Maybe that Digger hear us talk," Chahda suggested. "He tell Turk, and Turk think maybe he better suggest search to show he is number one on the level."

"Our Oriental wizard may have something there," Scotty agreed. "Anyway, Rick, we don't care who orders a search, as long as there is one, do we?"

"That's right," Rick said. "But I'll be happier when we're under way."

After dinner, the entire Spindrift party gathered in the pavilion. Dr. Warren had arrived in time to dine with them, and at the request of Hartson Brant was discussing their destination.

"I wish one of our people could go with you," he said. "I envy you the chance of seeing what Alta-Yuan is like. However, we are tied up at present in a half-dozen research projects."

"I'm going to feel rather responsible, acting as expedition archaeologist," Professor Gordon said. "After all, archaeology is only a hobby with me."

"You're much too modest," Dr. Warren smiled.

"Gordon hides his light under a bushel," Hartson Brant said. "Archaeology has been his hobby since college days. He used to spend his vacations in odd places, doing excavating and exploring. And during the war he managed to find time from his Navy duties to look around the islands a bit."

"Quite a bit," Dr. Warren agreed. "I think he'll find, however, that Kwangara will be his most interesting task to date. You doubtless know the history of Alta-Yuan—what we know of it—but perhaps I can sum it up for you."

"Please do," Zircon requested. "I was so involved in electronic problems that I neglected the other side of the project."

"Briefly," Dr. Warren began, "we first came across reference to the Kwangara temple on a plaque in the ruins of the Khmer civilization at Angkor, in French Cambodia. The plaque told of heavy storms that blew an explorer's ship off its course and carried it far to the east. The explorer discovered land, peopled by a race of white warriors. The warriors weren't very hospitable, according to the tale. The explorer and his friends narrowly escaped becoming Sunday dinners. The name of the land they found was Alta-Yuan, a name that was said to come from the great temple where these white warriors worshipped.

"There was no further mention of Alta-Yuan for a number of years. Then one of our expeditions to the Marianas stopped by Kwangara and found two interesting stones on a small peninsula. One was perfectly plain, no inscription on it. The other had been inscribed. The plain one was left, but the other was brought back. Not until a few months ago did we discover, by laborious translation, that it mentioned Alta-Yuan. We also discovered that these large stones were the outposts of a temple. The obvious conclusion was that we had found the fabled temple of Alta-Yuan, and that the main portion must be under the sea. If our calculations are correct, it is about 300 yards from the peninsula."

"What made Alta-Yuan sink under the sea?" Rick asked.

"We can only guess," Professor Gordon said. "Kwangara is right at the edge of what is known as a fault plane. There is a great deal of volcanic action in the area, and many earthquakes. Some such action doubtless dropped the major part of the land into the ocean and left only the highest spots. Kwangara is a single mountain peak, and near by is Little Kwangara, which is only a huge rock thrusting out of the ocean. In between the two is a valley. Alta-Yuan is somewhere in that valley."

Hobart Zircon asked, "Are the present inhabitants of Kwangara Polynesian?"

"Largely," Dr. Warren replied. "But they have a good deal of Mongoloid blood. A strange people. Since

Kwangara is very isolated, they've had little contact with civilization and they still cling to the old beliefs."

"Not head-hunting, I hope," Scotty said. "How come the war didn't bother them?"

"A great many islands had no contact with the war," Gordon answered. "Kwangara is too rocky for an airfield, too small for a base, and there are better ship anchorages in island groups not far away. Perhaps patrols landed and looked the place over, but there would be no reason for their remaining."

"It's funny for us to be hunting a lost temple after the things we've been working on," Rick mused. "It's a long way from the Tibet radar relay to a little hunk of real estate in the Pacific."

Hartson Brant laughed. "It is a change, Rick, but let's not underestimate the value of what we're doing. If the Submobile proves as excellent a salvage machine as we hope, it will be very useful. And new refinements can be added from our experiences on this trip." He smiled at Dr. Warren. "If we can help a fellow group of scientists while trying out our new equipment, that gives the expedition added value."

"I trust it will be a successful voyage," Dr. Warren said.

"Successful and peaceful," Rick added.

"There's no reason to think it won't be peaceful, is there?" Dr. Warren asked.

"No, sir, I guess not," Rick replied, but he had his fingers crossed.

CHAPTER VI

The High Seas

A school of flying fish broke water with a great thrashing of tails, heading away from the *Tarpon's* bow. Most of them plopped back into the waves after a flight of only a few yards, but Rick watched one glide between the wave crests for a good 200 feet.

"I used to thinking stories about flying fishes is fairy tales," Chahda remarked.

"They're real enough," Scotty said. "And watching them is about the only excitement you'll find this far out at sea."

"Dis fella him belong pigeon," Rick added, grinning. He was fast learning Otera's queer lingo, and that was what the native cook called flying fish.

The three boys leaned on the rail, letting the hot sun darken their skins. After twelve days at sea, dressed only in shorts and moccasins, Rick and Scotty were as brown as Chahda.

"Four more days to Kwangara," Rick mused. "I'm anxious to get there. This life on the ocean wave gets pretty dull." He had checked the chart after the noon position shots were figured. They were roughly halfway between Guam and the northern Palau Islands.

Otera came out of the galley and tossed a bucket of slops over the side. Rick hailed him.

"Otera! What fella belong us kai-kai tonight?"

The native cook grinned widely. "Got'm pigeon kai-kai fashion belong white man."

Translated from the *béché-de-mer*, that meant fried chicken. Rick had learned that "pigeon" meant anything with wings, from fish to airplanes. The boys were continually amused by Otera's language, and, since they were friendly, he had become fond of them.

At that moment Turk Mallane came out of the pilothouse, and Rick saw the instant change in Otera. The native cook's smile vanished, and he turned and almost ran back to the galley.

Turk's hard voice stopped him. "Otera!"

"Yes, marster?" the cook replied timidly.

"Rouse dis fella lap-lap belong you," Turk ordered, and, as he passed the boys, he muttered. "Filthy native swine. Wouldn't change clothes until they rotted off, unless told to."

Rick was thoughtful as he leaned on the rail again. Turk had ordered Otera to change his apron, which was slightly soiled, but not soiled enough to call forth such a comment. "There's a lad with a nice, friendly disposition," he stated.

Scotty grunted. "Remember I told you to ask me in a week whether I liked Turk or not? Okay, ask me."

"Well, do you?"

"No."

"Also," Chahda nodded.

Rick agreed with them. In the days since the *Tarpon* had sailed from Honolulu, Turk's affability had entirely vanished. He no longer made a pretence of friendship.

It was as though his good manners had been put on like a coat, and removed once they were at sea. But even though the captain was curt and irritable, no one could find fault with his seamanship. The trawler ran like a well-oiled machine. Nor was there any evidence of disloyalty. The search of the ship before leaving had proved negative. Everything was in order. And Turk had co-operated fully, almost eagerly, in aiding the scientists in the setting up of the diving equipment. Even though Professor Gordon had inspected the winches and their engines before leaving. Turk had insisted on personally tearing them down, cleaning them, inspecting each part, and putting them together again in tiptop working shape.

"Can't be too careful," he said shortly. "Lives will depend on those winches."

Digger Sears and the crew seemed to take their cue from Turk. They were all sullen, and spoke only when spoken to. As a result, the *Tarpon*, while a well-operated ship, could scarcely be called a jolly one.

Rick told himself that it didn't matter, as long as all went smoothly. With the passing of time he had come to believe that the incidents concerning the Japanese with the broken nose must have been unimportant co-incidence.

Professor Gordon called to him. "Rick, want to do a job for me?"

"Yes, sir. What is it?"

"That fluoride powder hasn't been mixed yet. If you want to tackle it now, I'll give you the proportions. Scotty and Chahda can help you collect the tooth powder."

Rick got the tins of fluoride powder and borrowed a set of kitchen measuring spoons from Otera, along with a pan for the mixing. Scotty and Chahda started collecting the individual cans of tooth powder from the cabins.

Scotty brought back a handful of powder cans and Rick sat down on the hatch cover next to the winches and started mixing according to the formula Gordon had given him.

On the open deck aft, Hartson Brant and Hobart Zircon were at work on the Submobile, completing the installations. The steel protection plates had been removed, showing the fused-quartz observation windows, one on the starboard side, the other on the nose, slightly to port. The scoop had been installed on one side of the blunt nose, and the scientists were just putting the extension arms in place on the other side, under the front observation window. Between the two salvage implements was the shining brass ball of the Sonoscope. A searchlight was set into the nose under the Sonoscope ball, its lens flush with the surface. One of the bronze propellers had been installed at the stern of the Submobile, while the others projected from the sides, two thirds of the way forward.

All of the exterior apparatus was operated by electric motors set within the hull. Levers controlled the propellers, while the scoop and salvage arms were operated from within by pistol grips with motor-control buttons in place of triggers.

Gordon had gone below decks to start the big Diesel generator. In a moment Hartson Brant climbed in through the open door of the Submobile and tested the arms. Rick stopped his mixing to watch. The extension arms moved forward, together, then individually. Then Mr. Brant moved them vertically, one at a time.

Satisfied with the test, the scientists started putting away their tools. "That does it," Zircon boomed, "except for final tests on the propellers. And that will have to wait until we get it into the water. We should have everything installed and checked tomorrow."

Chahda returned, carrying three cans of tooth powder. His usually pleasant face was angry. "All but Turk's," he said, handing the cans to Rick.

"What happened," Rick asked quickly.

"I start go into Turk's cabin to get his powder, and he sees me and yells 'Get out of there, you little beggar,' he says. So I do not get his can."

Rick started to stand up, anger burning in him. If Turk insisted that no one got into his cabin, he could at least be civil about it.

"Please say nothing," Chahda said quickly. "No trouble. It is Turk's cabin. He says don't go in, so I don't. That is all."

"He's right," Scotty said. "No use making an issue out of it."

Rick subsided, knowing that they were right. In a few days the trawler would arrive at Kwangara and the experiment would get under way. An open feud with the captain wouldn't make things any easier.

Scotty and Chahda helped him pour the mixture of fluoride and tooth powder back into the individual cans. There was a lot of the mixture left over, and a full can of fluoride powder. Rick called to Professor Gordon, who was inspecting the packing of one of the propeller shafts.

"No use wasting it," Gordon said, when Rick had shown him the surplus powder. "See if you can find a can with a cover. Maybe Otera has a coffee jar or something."

Dewey and Hughey, two of the crew, were in the galley drinking coffee. The sailors looked up as Rick entered, then looked away, ignoring his presence. They hadn't spoken more than ten words during the entire trip.

"Do you have an empty coffee jar?" Rick asked Otera. Then, at the cook's puzzled look, he tried to put it into *bêché-de-mer*. "You gottem one fella box him belong coffee?"

Otera nodded. Silently he went to a cupboard and brought out a clean coffee jar with a screw top. Rick thanked him and went out on deck, very thoughtful.

There had been a change in Otera since leaving port. At first, he had been perpetually smiling, with some weird little tune on his lips as he worked. He still smiled, when there was no one around except the boys. But when Turk, Digger, or the crew were near he was quiet and nervous as a frightened rabbit.

"He's scared stiff," Rick surmised. "But of what?" Of being beaten, probably. Digger was a heavy-handed mate, although he had shown no outward signs of brutality since Hartson Brant had spoken to him. Turk and the three crew members were also tough customers. Rick wouldn't put it past them to take a whack at the cook if anything displeased them. He resolved to keep his eyes open for any sign that Otera was being secretly kicked into submission.

He put the extra mixture of tooth powder and fluoride into the coffee jar and screwed the cover on tightly, then took it below to stow with the camping supplies and medical equipment. Scotty and Chahda were returning the tooth-powder cans to the cabins of their owners.

A roar from the deck brought Rick topside again. Turk Mallane was bellowing orders.

"All hands! Smartly, blast it! Secure all loose gear and batten down!"

Rick ran out on deck and saw everyone galvanized into hurried activity. Astern, a line squall was bearing down on them, a solid line of black clouds against the sky.

Hartson Brant called, "Help us with the hatch cover, quickly!"

Rick and Scotty ran to him. Chahda was helping Professor Gordon get tools and equipment below decks.

"The wiring of the Sonoscope is exposed," Zircon boomed. "We must get the hatch on or it will get wet." The big scientist was working at the block and tackle that had been rigged for the hatch cover, a 200-pound circle of heavy steel, much like a manhole cover. The hatch cover had to be lifted with the block and tackle, then pushed into place over a circle of bolts that projected from the Submobile.

Rick helped Zircon untangle the block and tackle while Scotty jumped and caught the dangling hook. In a moment the tackle was free, and Scotty slipped the hook through the ring of the massive cover.

"Now," Zircon bellowed. He threw his weight on the rope while Hartson Brant and the two boys guided the cover toward the circle of bolts. The cover struck, bounced off, tearing loose from their hands.

And the squall struck!

The trawler shuddered under the combined force of wind and sea and rocked up on her beam ends. She dove deep, and her nose buried in a sudden swell. Water cascaded down the deck.

Rick jumped to help Zircon, water running around his ankles. The wind whipped the top from the near-by waves, and salt spray and rain slashed into his face.

The heavy cover was dancing in the air, just short of the fringe of bolts. Zircon braced himself and tugged, Rick helping. Then the trawler buried her nose in another swell and water crashed down the deck. Rick tried for a more secure footing, and the rubber soles of his moccasins betrayed him. His feet shot out from under him and a sudden roll of the ship threw him heavily against the steel cradle of the Submobile. He was on his feet instantly, feeling pain shoot through him. He ignored it and jumped back to where Zircon was holding fast to the rope.

The trawler climbed to the top of a swell and hesitated for a heartbeat before plunging into the trough. The brief hesitation was just enough for Scotty and Hartson Brant to slide the hatch cover over the bolts. Scotty held it in place while the scientist spun on wing nuts.

"All right," Hartson Brant yelled above the noise of crashing water. "Get to cover!"

Rick and Zircon let go of the rope, and Rick started for the companionway that led below decks. His leg buckled under him and he fell heavily against Zircon.

The big scientist scooped him up and carried him to shelter, Scotty and Hartson Brant hurrying anxiously behind.

CHAPTER VII

The Stowaway

RICK sat on the edge of his bunk and examined a leg that was already turning purple. He had struck an edge of the steel cradle with the big muscle of his thigh. It hurt like the dickens, but it wasn't serious.

"I saw you hit," Scotty said, "but you were on your feet right away, so I didn't think you had been hurt."

"There wasn't time for me to find out," Rick said ruefully.

"We can be thankful it wasn't more serious," Hartson Brant said. "It will be painful for a while, Rick."

Chahda grinned. "Also, it will be pretty, like sunset."

"You and your Hindu philosophy," Scotty scoffed. "Would you be as cheerful if it was your leg?"

"No," Chahda said truthfully. "I just try cheer up Rick."

"Help me up, don't cheer me up," Rick said. "I want to walk around a little so it won't stiffen up on me."

"Good idea," Zircon said. "Help him out on deck, Scotty. The squall is past."

Rick took a turn around the deck, then sat down on the hatch cover. The pain had subsided to an ache and he could walk with only a slight limp. The squall had vanished over the horizon, leaving the air moist and cool.

"Odd how those pocket-size storms come and go," Gordon said. "Hello . . . what's up?"

Turk Mallane was striding toward them, his face dark with anger. He held up a piece of black material festooned with wires. Rick recognized it instantly as a radio tube, the glass broken.

"Fine piece of work," Turk said angrily. "The cover was off the radiophone box and the stupid fool at the wheel didn't cover it up when the storm broke. This is the result—a smashed tube. A pair of field glasses fell into the box."

Hartson Brant examined the broken thing. "The final output tube," he said. "Do you have a replacement, Captain?"

"No," Turk said. "Thanks to Digger. I told him to pick up some spares and thought he had. It's my own fault for leaving details to someone else."

"That means no ship-to-shore communication," Scotty said with a glance at Rick.

"I don't know as it matters much," Zircon stated. "We haven't used the radiophone and there would be no occasion, unless we were in distress, which is unlikely. Don't worry about it, Captain."

"Thanks," Turk said gruffly. "I was afraid you'd be upset."

Rick watched the broad-shouldered figure as Turk went back to the pilothouse. "I don't like it," he said. "We should have brought our own radio."

"There's no need," Gordon replied. "As Hobart pointed out, we wouldn't need it except in case of distress."

Then Otera arrived with a large platter of fried chicken and the matter was forgotten in the pleasant business of eating.

Gentle breathing from the bunks next to him and above him told Rick that Scotty and Chahda were sound asleep. He had been asleep, too, but not soundly. The ache of his bruised leg had awakened him.

He shifted the leg to a more comfortable position and stared into the darkness. Outside the wooden hull the gurgle of the water was pleasant, and the throb of the Diesel engines was muffled.

Three more days to Kwangara. He hoped they would pass quickly. He was anxious to make his first dive in the Submobile, to get his first look at the lost temple of Alta-Yuan, buried for centuries beneath the sea. His active imagination drew a picture of it as it must have been before the water swallowed it.

Presently he tired of trying to picture what it would be like when they found it. He decided that he was hungry. He hadn't eaten much of the delicious fried chicken, because the pain in his leg had robbed him of his normal appetite.

He swung to the deck and tested his footing. The leg was a bit stiff, but he could walk all right. He slipped into his moccasins, and went out the cabin door, and turned toward the refrigerator room. There was no need for lights. He knew just where everything was.

In the refrigerator room the tiny glow of the pilot light showed him the door handle. He swung it open, shivering in the sudden rush of icy air. The pilot light, which showed that the freezing unit was operating, gave enough glow so that he could locate the apple barrel. He found a good-sized one and swung the door shut, silently so that he wouldn't awaken anyone.

The apple was too cold to bite into. He stood in the passageway and rubbed it between his hands, warming it. Turk Mallane, grouch though he might be, certainly knew how to stock a ship.

He lifted the apple to take a bite and suddenly halted. There was a clatter from up forward, behind the door that led to the paint locker. Something had fallen. Curious, he walked over, silent in his moccasins, and threw the door open.

A dark form hurtled forward and drove him violently against the metal door jamb. Rick let out a yell of surprised fright, then a grunt as powerful arms locked around his pyjamaed waist. Before he could gather his wits and fight back, the unexpected assailant had his arms tied fast in a judo hold.

Rick kicked out, and his moccasin drove into soft flesh. There was a grunt, then an elbow caught him under the chin and he saw stars. He squirmed, but the grip tightened painfully. He threw his weight forward, his legs driving, and gained a little room.

Lights flashed on in the passageway and he caught a quick glimpse of Chahda, his hand on the switch, and Scotty, jumping headlong through the door.

The man's hands dropped from Rick's arms as he whirled to meet Scotty's charge. Then there was the unbelievable, incredible spectacle of Scotty flying through the air, to land with a stunning crash against the refrigerator!

Rick rushed, his shoulder low, and took the man in the side. They catapulted into the passageway, and the stranger gave a catlike twist that brought him on top.

Then Chahda stepped in, an iron meat hook in his hand. He brought it down sharply and the stranger collapsed in a heap on top of Rick.

Rick pushed the inert form aside and got to his feet, a little dizzy. Scotty stood up at the same time, rubbing his head and with a look of dismayed surprise on his face.

Chahda, still holding the hook—one that had been used to hang a side of beef in the refrigerator—bent and rolled the man over.

Rick stared at the face, and somehow he wasn't surprised.

It was the Japanese with the broken nose!

The passageway was full now, the scientists and the crew hurrying toward the sound of the fighting.

"What is it?" Hartson Brant asked. "Are you all right, boys?"

"We're okay," Rick answered.

Zircon stared down at the unconscious man on the deck. "Rick," he exclaimed, "isn't that . . ."

"Yes, sir," Rick answered. "It's the one we got the picture of."

Turk Mallane pushed his way to the fore and stared down at the Japanese.

"Who found him?" he demanded.

"I did," Rick said. "I went to the reefer for an apple, and I heard a noise from the paint locker. I thought something had fallen, so I went to look—and he jumped me."

Scotty went into the paint locker room, turning on the lights. In a moment he returned. "I found where he was hiding," he stated. "There's a false wall in there. That's why we missed him when we searched. I spotted it this time because he left the boards pulled out.

Professor Gordon had bent over the Japanese. "He's coming to, I think. Someone gave him a hard belt."

"That was Chahda," Rick said.

The Japanese groaned and opened his eyes. Gordon moved back and he sat up.

"On your feet," Turk Mallane growled. He lifted the Japanese upright and let him lean against a bulkhead. "Now," he said. "What are you doing here?"

Beady, expressionless eyes flicked from face to face.

"Talk," Digger Sears threatened, "or we'll bash you again."

"None of that," Turk snapped. "Get back to the bridge, Digger. Come on, fellow. What are you doing here?"

The man shrugged and said something in Japanese.

"Perhaps he can't speak English," Rick suggested.

"Possible," Hartson Brant said, "but highly improbable. He just doesn't want to speak."

Rick blurted suddenly, "Is your name Asamo?"

There was a small flicker of intelligence deep in the man's eyes, then he was impassive again. But Turk Mallane whirled and demanded, "What do you know . . . what makes you think his name is Asamo?"

"Yes, Rick, what is this?" Hartson asked.

Rick explained about the scrap of paper they had found in their cabin.

"Have you heard the name before?" Rick asked Turk.

"It sounds familiar," Turk admitted. "But that doesn't mean anything. Many Japanese names sound alike. I think the important question is, how did he manage to remain hidden for so long?"

"No one has been in the paint locker," Scotty put in. "And that false bulkhead made a good hiding place. He could have gotten plenty of food by taking fruit and leftovers from the refrigerator.''

Rick said, ''The big question is what is he doing aboard? What does he want?''

No one had an answer to that.

''Well, even if he is aboard without permission,'' Hartson Brant said, ''we can't leave him in that hole for ever. We'll lock him in at night and let him out with a guard in the daytime. I'd like to know what he is doing here, but if he won't talk, we can't make him.''

''There's no point in standing here,'' Turk put in. ''I'll see that he's locked up for the night. Perhaps morning will throw some light on the deal.'' He motioned to the Japanese.

The man went sullenly. Rick and Scotty followed as Turk walked into the paint locker with him. As Scotty had said, one side of the locker had a false wall, the boards pulled out now. There was just room for a man to stretch out in there.

Turk went through the man's clothes swiftly and came up with a jackknife and a paper of matches. ''He's not armed,'' he said.

The door was normally unlocked, but it had a regular door lock. Turk produced a ring of keys and turned the bolt. ''I don't know as we've anything to fear from him. He can't do anything to the ship without hurting himself in the bargain. But I'll have the watch keep an eye on him.''

In a few moments order was restored and the boys were in their bunks, the lights out.

''He scared the starch out of me,'' Rick admitted. ''I didn't expect to find anyone when I opened the door. Wonder why he jumped me like that?''

"You startled him," Scotty said. "He probably heard you go to the refrigerator, then he heard the door close and thought you'd gone back to your cabin. I imagine he was on his way to get a bite to eat. Then, when you suddenly opened the door, he jumped."

"He was more scared than you, I bet," Chahda added.

"I'd like to meet that character on even terms." Scotty didn't sound happy. "He took me by surprise. I didn't expect a judo expert."

Chahda chuckled. "For a minute I think maybe Scotty is learning to fly like bird."

"That's the meat-hook kid talking," Rick laughed. "Seriously, what do you think he's doing here?"

Neither Scotty nor Chahda had any suggestions.

"Maybe finding our friend will put a stop to what-ever he had planned," Rick said.

"Maybe," Scotty said pessimistically. "But don't bet on it."

"Watch out, Asamo," Chahda reminded.

"That's another side to the puzzle," Rick agreed. "What does it mean? Is it our new friend's name? Did the scrap of paper get into our cabin by mistake, or was it a warning? And who wrote it?"

Scotty laughed, but there was no humour in it. "A lot of questions, and not a single answer."

"Tomorrow answers, maybe," Chahda said.

"I have a hunch," Rick replied slowly, "that a lot of tomorrows will go by before we get the answers to all this."

CHAPTER VIII

Kwangara Island

THE *Tarpon* rode the long Pacific swells gently, her engines turning over just enough to give her rudder control.

Rick strained his eyes to see through the darkness to where the high bulk of land made a deeper blackness against the sky.

"It will be daylight soon," Scotty said.

The Spindrift party was gathered on the afterdeck of the trawler, waiting for the first glimmer of dawn to show them their destination. They had arrived off Kwangara in the late hours of night, and all hands had gotten dressed, too excited to sleep any longer.

Otera appeared with glasses of fruit juice, which were gratefully accepted. He passed the juice around in silence, then hurried back to the galley. Questioning the cook had brought no results. Rick was sure he knew something, but fright sealed his lips.

Nor had anyone else admitted knowledge of the stowaway, or his reason for being aboard. The Japanese himself was taking the whole thing very calmly. He had not spoken a word, nor did they expect him to. By day he had been permitted on deck, up in the bow where the steersman could keep an eye on him. At night he had been secured in the paint locker. Apparently entirely content, he had spent his days staring out to sea and enjoying the sunlight.

Rick's head was tired from trying to think of reasons for his presence. There was nothing he could do about it, except to keep his eyes open. By unspoken agreement, the entire Spindrift group was watchful, each seeking some solution to the puzzle. Scotty had taken his rifle from its storage place, and it was never far from his side.

Turk Mallane came by and spoke cheerfully to the silent group.

"Dawn in about fifteen minutes. What are the plans? We won't get the Submobile into the water today, I'm thinking."

Hartson Brant answered him. "Not today, Captain. We'll set up camp first thing, then mount the sound ball on the bow and see if we can't locate the temple. If we succeed, we can make our first test dives to-morrow."

Rick pondered the change in Turk. As the trawler had neared Kwangara, the broad-shouldered captain had regained his good humour. Perhaps he was one of those men who turn irritable under stress and regain their usual poise when the crisis is over. Rick didn't think that was the answer, however. Turk's friendliness wasn't genuine.

As the first streaks of daylight turned the eastern sky pink, Otera came again with coffee and sandwiches. Rick leaned against the rail with the rest of the Spindrift party, and tried to pierce the darkness that still lay over Kwangara.

Little by little, as the sky lightened, they made out details. They had been running back and forth a half mile away from a small island that seemed to be mostly a pyramid of rock thrusting out of the sea, a few trees around its base. That would be Little Kwangara. Beyond it, perhaps 2,000 yards farther on, was the high bulk of Kwangara itself. As full daylight came, Rick saw that it was a green-clad mountain that ended in a rocky cone. Kwangara had evidently been a volcano.

From the bridge came a sharp order and the engines turned faster. Turk himself took the wheel as the trawler pointed its bow toward the larger island.

Rick saw the white line of surf that marked the reef. He could see clearly now that they were heading for a spit of land that thrust out from Kwangara. Turk took them right up to the reef and through the passage as the leadsman sang out his depths. They dropped anchor in eight fathoms just 100 feet from the tip of the small peninsula.

Behind the spit of land, the island rose sharply, covered with a seemingly impenetrable maze of trees and underbrush. From somewhere inland, a bird cry made a harsh welcome that only intensified the silence.

The three scientists bent over their chart, and the boys joined them. The spit of land was clearly marked. It was one of three flat places. At the south end of the island was a plain where a native village, probably the only one, had been indicated. At the northwestern tip was another plain marked as marshland. Otherwise, the island was mountainous. The highest peak was marked as 1,200 feet.

The crew was already busy lowering one of the two whaleboats. Turk joined the scientific party. "I know you're anxious to get ashore. I'd like to go with you."

"Of course," Hartson Brant said.

Turk turned and gave orders to Digger Sears, who had followed him from the bridge. "Keep that stow-away locked up until we get back. And start rigging the bow platform for the sound gear."

It took only a moment to get aboard the whaleboat and cast off. Turk himself took one oar, and Scotty the other. After a short pull the sand grated under them.

From the beach the small peninsula rose very gradu-ally for about 200 feet. Then the wall of the jungle began, its edge as clearly defined as though a giant's knife had shorn the foliage. Scotty, rifle in hand, joined Rick in his examination of their new base. The spit of land was cov-ered with knee-high grass, right up to the jungle's edge.

"Wonder why the jungle stops there?" Rick asked.

Professor Gordon answered him. "There's bedrock under us, with just a thin layer of soil. Too thin to support anything but grass. But look over here, boys."

They followed him to a table of stone. It was about three feet high, six feet long and four wide, obviously carved by hand from a huge piece of volcanic rock.

"That's the stone Dr. Warren told us about," Rick said. "It's the edge of what used to be the temple!" The sight of the stone excited him. It was the first tangible evidence of the presence of Alta-Yuan. He looked out to sea, past the trawler. The rest of the temple was out there, somewhere. . . .

Scotty was still looking toward the jungle, bent forward a little, his head turned as though he strained to hear something.

"Did you hear a noise?" Rick asked.

"No," Scotty said. His voice was hushed. "That's just it. Listen, everyone."

The scientists stopped talking and silence pressed in on them. It was a living, uncanny silence, as though the whole island held its breath. Unaccountably, Rick shivered.

"I don't like it," Scotty said. His voice was lost in the stillness. "A jungle is usually the noisiest place on earth."

"You're right," Professor Gordon agreed. "Full of birds and insects and small animals and all kinds of un-explained noises."

Chahda gave a visible shudder. "It is like the Towers of Silence in Bombay, where Parsees bury the dead," he whispered. "I think is smelling the same, too, like much death."

Rick nodded. There was a strange odour, of lush tropic growth and alien flowers, of decay and wet muskiness.

"Nonsense," Hobart Zircon boomed. "We'll get our-selves into a fine state of nerves. It's simply that we're used to the bustle and noise aboard ship. Isn't that right, Captain Mallane?"

"Sure," Turk agreed. "Your ears are still full of the engine noise. You got so used to it aboard ship that you'd no longer noticed. But ashore, it makes everything seem unnaturally quiet."

Rick looked at Scotty and saw him shrug. Scotty wasn't convinced.

Chahda, who had started prowling through the long grass near the table stone, suddenly called. "I found a thing!"

The others hurried to his side, and Rick saw a fragment of carved, broken stone about six inches square. Before it was a small pile of fresh fruit, coconuts, and bits of carved wood. A stick, thrust into the ground, carried a small bit of white bark at its tip. A trampled path led through the grass from the pile to the jungle.

"Natives," Turk said in a tone of disgust.

Before anyone could make a move to stop him, his foot had scattered the pile of fruit.

The scientists exclaimed, but Turk added hurriedly, "If you're going to camp here, it's best to discourage the beasts right off. You don't want them around."

"But we do!" Gordon stated. "I'm curious to see what they're like. I've even brought equipment for making cranial measurements."

"Yes," Hartson Brant agreed. "Please let any native stuff alone that we may find, Captain. We want them to be friendly."

Turk growled agreement.

Rick missed Scotty. He turned and saw him near the edge of the jungle, his rifle held in the curve of his arm.

"We're being watched," Scotty said quietly. "I felt it before, but I wasn't sure until Turk kicked that stuff. Whoever is in there didn't like it."

"How do you know?" Rick asked curiously.

Scotty shrugged. "I just know, that's all. I feel it."

"Also," said Chahda, who had joined them.

That was evidence enough for Rick. He had had experience before with Scotty's well-developed intuition. Scotty had "jungle sense," acquired during his service in the Marines. Chahda's upbringing, living by his wits in the slums of Bombay, had given him the same extra perception.

Watching the dense wall of jungle, Rick had the weird sensation of eyes watching his every move. Abruptly he turned away.

The scientists, however, were too enrapt by their examination of the carved fragment Chahda had discovered to notice anything unusual.

"It is evidently a portion of a head," Gordon was saying as the boys rejoined them. "However, I'm not prepared to say what kind of head. It might be a lion, a dog, or a snake."

Turk Mallane demanded impatiently, "Well, do we get going? I'll have your camping stuff brought ashore if you say the word, and you can have camp pitched by noon."

"By all means," Hartson Brant said.

The next hours were busy ones. With all hands helping, the camp equipment was brought ashore and "Camp Spindrift," as Scotty named it, began to take shape.

Rick found time to ask Scotty: "What do you think of us camping ashore like this and leaving only Turk and company aboard ship—not to mention our Japanese pal?"

Scotty thought it over. "I think it's all right," he said finally. "After all, what could they do? They wouldn't run off and leave us. They could be tracked down too easily once Dr. Warren's people decided we'd been gone too long without any word and sent a rescue plane."

"Maybe they want the equipment," Rick suggested.

"They can't operate it," Scotty pointed out. "And it would do them no good to damage it. If that was what they wanted, they could have done it long ago. Besides, we haven't a thing on Turk, except that he was grouchy at sea."

"Don't forget the Jap," Rick said.

"He's a puzzle," Scotty agreed. "But what can he do? If he had wanted to damage the equipment, he could easily have done it before you found him. And he can't hurt the boat without sinking himself."

The answers echoed Rick's thoughts, nevertheless he was uneasy. "All we can do is let nature take its course," he said. "That's a futile way of doing things, but what else is there?"

"Nothing," Scotty said. "Come on, help me with this tent."

The two pyramid tents were erected with the jointed poles and steel tent pegs that had been brought along. Three Army cots were placed in each, complete with mattress pads, blankets, and mosquito nets. A water bag was set up on a tripod of poles, to be filled daily from the ship's supply.

Meanwhile, Hobart Zircon and Professor Gordon had set up the camp's electrical system. Several storage batteries operated a small converter that produced 110 volts. A one-cylinder, gasoline charging unit would keep up the voltage in the batteries. Lights were strung within the tents and on a line that stretched between them. In the tent assigned to the boys was placed a two-unit electric plate and an electric percolator in case a meal was wanted ashore. Professor Gordon took the medical supplies and his ultraviolet sterilizer into his own tent.

"This spit of land seems healthy enough," he said. "We may not even need to use the DDT and the sterilizer."

By lunchtime, the place was shipshape and ready for occupancy. Rick was pleased as he looked around at the little camp. While the space ashore would be needed for the material they found on the sea bottom, one of the main reasons for the camp was that none of the Spindrift party especially enjoyed living in the crowded, stuffy quarters aboard ship.

As they prepared to go back to the ship for lunch, Scotty asked Hartson Brant, "How about a guard for t. e camp, sir? If we leave it, the natives might steal everything in sight."

"We'll fix that," Professor Gordon stated. He rummaged in a supply box and found a coil of strong twine. Then he tore a white handkerchief into half a dozen strips. While Rick watched, wondering, Gordon and Scotty strung the twine across the peninsula right at the edge of the jungle. Then Gordon hung the strips of handkerchief at intervals.

"Now," Gordon stated, "the peninsula is safe."

"Sure enough." Scotty grinned. "I'd forgotten about that."

"We're making the camp tabu," Gordon explained. "Did you notice the strip of white bark on the stick next to the pile of offerings? That's proof that these people cling to the old beliefs."

Rick looked at the strips of white handkerchief with disbelief.

"Do you mean that little string will actually keep them away?"

"It's the mark of the tabu," Gordon affirmed. "It has been for centuries. They firmly believe that to break a tabu means death. They won't risk it."

"It actually works," Scotty assured Rick. "You'll see."

"I'll have to see," Rick stated. "When do we get a demonstration?"

Scotty looked at the forbidding wall of jungle behind the line of white strips. There was worry in his eyes as he said: "Maybe sooner than you think."

CHAPTER IX

Searching by Sound

DIGGER SEARS, acting on Turk's instructions, had rigged a platform on the bow of the trawler. After lunch, Hartson Brant directed the placing of the sound equipment on the platform.

A rounded brass dome, about eighteen inches in diameter, was lowered into the water under the trawler's bow, then securely bolted to the plank platform. Hobart Zircon opened a large metal case, exposing a complicated control board that had a circular screen, a loud-speaker, and an illuminated scale. A cable was secured to a socket in the control box, and its other end plugged into the brass dome. Then a power cable was attached to the deck generator outlet.

"We'll cover the entire channel between here and Little Kwangara," Hartson Brant instructed Turk. "I'll depend on you to take sightings with the pelorus whenever we locate anything on the bottom. Professor Gordon will sketch the depth curves."

"Right," Turk agreed. He shouted instructions to up anchor, and the trawler moved slowly out through the reef opening. As they cleared the reef, Hartson Brant turned a knob and the panel lit up.

On the circular screen, a hand like that of a clock began its slow sweep. The illuminated scale showed dancing points of light. As another switch was turned, the loud-speaker began to give out a rapid beep-beep of sound.

Rick watched, fascinated. He knew the theory of the thing, but he had never before seen it in operation. The brass ball was sending out bursts of supersonic waves, inaudible to the human ear. As they struck bottom, the sound waves were reflected and picked up again by the apparatus. The illuminated scale automatically showed the time of the echo, measured in feet instead of seconds. The beep-beep noise was the initial sound impulse, translated into audible sound, and followed closely by the returning echo.

As the water deepened, the space between the beeps grew more pronounced, and Hartson Brant began to read the depths aloud.

"50, 50, 55, 60, 58, 57, 60, 65, 69. . . ."

Rick had a mental picture of the bottom as his father droned out the readings. A gradual slope, then a small hill, and the bottom dropped more sharply. . . . He sighted across the bow and saw that Turk was heading slowly out to sea at right angles to the shore of Kwangara.

The deepest spot was almost 1,600 feet, close to the small island known as Little Kwangara. Turk brought the trawler even with the small island, turned her sharply and headed back on a parallel course.

The trawler had made four such runs before Hartson Brant found anything of interest. He called sharply, "I have something. Gordon, get this." He read off figures showing a sharp, irregular rise and fall on the sea bottom.

Rick sighted across the stern. They were about 1,000 feet from Camp Spindrift, in 600 feet of water. Their line of travel was between the spit of land and the southern tip of Little Kwangara.

Every person aboard, except for the Japanese, who was locked up, and Turk and one seaman who were in the pilothouse, had gathered to watch over Hartson Brant's shoulder.

Rick grinned at Scotty. Even Otera, Digger, and the other two crewmen were excited.

Turk stepped out on deck, and he was grinning from ear to ear. "Shall I make another run over that spot?"

"Please," Hartson Brant said. He looked up from the control panel. "There's certainly something there."

Turk swung the trawler and headed back. Again the sound equipment picked up irregular echoes. Gordon was jotting them down, and making a diagram from the distances given.

Four times more the trawler ran over the spot, on a slightly different course each time. As they ran across for the last time, Gordon gave an exultant shout.

"It's the temple! It must be! That last run gave me the dimensions. Listen: It's almost square, roughly 100 feet on a side. And there must be a wide wall around it, about ten feet high. I don't know how wide, because the gear isn't that sensitive, but it must be pretty wide, since it registers."

Turk turned the trawler over to Digger and joined the scientists. "It's the doggondest thing I've seen," he exclaimed. "They didn't have this stuff when I was doing salvage. It certainly pegs the bottom, doesn't it?"

There was no doubting Turk's genuine enthusiasm. The captain was as pleased over the finding of the temple as any of the Spindrift party. Rick began to like Turk a little better.

"Did you get bearings?" Hartson Brant asked.

"To the inch," Turk boasted. "I can take you to any corner of the place you want."

"Fine," Zircon boomed. "Well, Harston, what now?"

"I think we had better continue charting the bottom," Mr. Brant said. "There may be other portions of the temple, or perhaps another building somewhere around."

"Okay," Turk said agreeably. "Here we go."

As Turk ran the trawler back and forth, the depth contour of the bottom took shape. The sea bottom sloped gradually from Kwangara until it reached a maximum depth of 1,600 feet about 2,000 feet from Little Kwangara. Then it rose abruptly to Little Kwangara reef.

Nothing unusual showed on the sound gear. The beeps continued, only the space between them showing the gradual bottom change. Then, 300 yards off the southern tip of Little Kwangara, Hartson Brant suddenly turned the speaker volume high. The echo pinged sharply.

"Strange," the scientist said. "Did you hear that? Captain, run that spot again, please."

Turk did so, and the character of the beeps changed sharply.

"Metal," Zircon exclaimed. "Almost certainly metal."

The trawler swung again, and Gordon jotted down Mr. Brant's readings. "750, 750, 720, 720, 750, 750, 700, 670. . . ."

"Sheer off!" Hartson Brant called suddenly. "We're running on a steep-to shore!"

The trawler's nose swung sharply about as Turk spun the wheel. He headed back to Kwangara, then came out on deck. "What's up?"

"An underwater cliff," Hartson Brant explained. "I didn't want to risk going closer until we found out how close it comes to the surface. Gordon, what do the figures show?"

Gordon examined his sketch. "The bottom rises abruptly, shelves off for about 300 feet, then rises again to a steep cliff. The shelf is at 750 feet, and there's something on it, about 30 feet high, and pretty large. A ship, almost certainly."

He looked at the interested faces around him. "Did we say that war didn't come to Kwangara? I'd say at least one ship was sunk here, unless some merchantman struck that cliff, sank herself, and came to rest on that ledge."

"Perhaps we can investigate when we've finished with the temple," Zircon suggested.

"You never know where you'll find wrecks these days," Turk Mallane said. "But I'll tell you this. That one didn't hit that underwater cliff."

"How do you know that?" Zircon asked quickly.

"I can tell by the colour of the water that the cliff doesn't come close enough to the surface to be a menace. I'd say the ship was sunk." There was ill-concealed excitement in the way Turk grinned at them. "Funny, isn't it?" he chuckled. "I'm as geared up over this business as any of you."

"Rick, get the chart, please, and give it to the captain," Hartson Brant requested. "Will you transfer your pelorus sightings to our chart as well as your own, Captain? I think we can go back to our anchorage now. We've found what we want."

Rick took the chart into the pilothouse and watched Turk transfer his sightings, placing both the temple and the sunken ship in their exact locations.

"Haven't enjoyed anything so much since we found the old *Havana Girl* in 250 feet off the Isle of Pines," Turk said jovially. "You're lucky to be along on a trip like this, lad."

"I guess I am," Rick said shortly. He couldn't forget that Turk had been snarling at everyone only a few days past. He didn't like anyone who changed his colours so often.

As the trawler headed back to the anchorage, Rick joined Scotty at the rail.

"I wonder what that ship is?" Scotty mused. "A merchantman, or a warship? Japanese or American? Or maybe British?"

"We'll probably never know," Rick said. "Unless there's time to make a few dives and investigate when we're through with the temple." He looked at his watch. "Gosh, it's suppertime. We've been at this all afternoon."

"I don't need a watch," Scotty said with a grin. "My stomach tells me when it's time to eat."

Chahda, who had helped Zircon to disconnect the sound equipment, came and stood beside them.

"Turk very happy," the Hindu boy told them. "He stands in pilothouse and hums like happy bumblebee."

"Not only Turk," Scotty added. "Even Digger is grinning like a contented horse."

Rick watched two of the seamen standing by the anchor, ready to let go when they were inside the reef. "Dewey, Hughey, and Lewey, too," he agreed. It was strange, but the afternoon's work had changed the entire atmosphere of the ship.

"I haven't seen our Japanese friend," Rick commented, "but if he's like the rest, he's probably whistling 'The Prisoner's Song' and feeling happy about the whole thing."

But if the trawler echoed excited happiness from all hands, the island itself hadn't changed. The Spindrift group went ashore in twilight and turned on the power system, to give them lights while getting ready for bed. The hum of the generator was loud in the stillness, and even the strong light of the bulbs seemed to be lost in the darkness at the edge of the jungle.

Rick noted that Scotty's rifle was never far from his friend's hand. He asked quietly, "Nervous?"

"Yes," Scotty answered bluntly. "It's too quiet."

"Much quiet," Chahda agreed. "I not liking."

Then, when they were in their bunks with the power turned off, the silence pressed in with even more intensity. Rick felt stifled under his mosquito net, but he knew he shouldn't open it. He lay awake, tense with listening for some sound that never came.

CHAPTER X

A Threat from the Jungle

RICK awoke to a stir of activity. The scientists were already up and dressed, and he could see the crew at work aboard the trawler. They were rigging the heavy booms and winding the salvage cable on the smaller of the two winches.

Scotty and Chahda got into their clothes and came out of the tent to stand beside him.

"Something's happened," Scotty said suddenly. "Listen!"

"Noises," Chahda exclaimed. "The woods is come to life!"

Rick listened, then walked toward the jungle's edge. As he approached a white cockatoo rose into the air with a screech. It was true, the jungle had come to life! He could hear bird songs from the deep woods, and once a crashing through the underbrush as some animal ran past.

"Wild boar," Scotty guessed. "Nothing else in these islands big enough to make noise like that."

"But what has happened?" Rick asked, bewildered.

"Our friends have gone back to their village, I suspect," Scotty replied. "What do you think, Chahda?"

"Also. Yesterday they watch, and last night. This morning they go."

The scientists had noticed the change, too. Professor Gordon shook his head. "I'm at a complete loss. This is the first time I've ever come across unfriendly natives. Usually they come right into camp and start bartering for fresh fruit or fish."

"Anyway," Rick said with a glance at the dangling pieces of white handkerchief, "they haven't crossed the line."

"They won't," Scotty assured him.

Out on the trawler, Turk greeted them heartily and showed them what had been accomplished. The booms were rigged for operation and the electric power cable had been unwrapped from its protecting burlap and lay ready. The main cable and the salvage cable had been wound on their separate winches during the early part of the trip.

"The rest is up to you," he said, smiling. "My part's done."

"Well done," Hartson Brant complimented him. "You're a very efficient skipper, Captain Mallane."

Turk smiled his thanks. "I've let the stowaway come topside for a while." He pointed to where the Japanese was taking his ease near the galley. "We'll put him back in the locker when we're ready to start operations. Otera has your breakfast ready."

It was a quick breakfast, because everyone was anxious to start. With Turk and Digger interested observers, work on the Submobile began.

Rick and Scotty went to the supply room and brought out small cylinders of oxygen. Chahda crawled into the Submobile and put air-purifying chemicals in place.

To Turk's questions, Rick explained: "We make our own air. There's a steady supply of oxygen from the tanks. Then, we use calcium chloride for absorbing the moisture in the air, and soda lime for absorbing the carbon dioxide. Two bottles of oxygen are big enough to supply two men for ten hours."

Meanwhile, the scientists were making a recheck of the four danger points where pressure might leak through. These were at the propeller shafts, and at the top stuffing box through which the power cable passed. A check showed the salvage apparatus and the Sonoscope operating.

Finally, the main cable was attached to the lift ring on top of the Submobile and the winch rechecked. Turk already had steam up in the big Diesel-steam winch.

The last step was to unbolt the Submobile cradle from the deck, and as Rick and Scotty did so with huge wrenches, the trawler started for the passage through the reef.

Rick arose with the last bolt in his hand as they passed the reef. He wiped sweat from his forehead and grinned at his father. "All set, Dad."

"Fine, Rick. Got your camera?"

"I'll get it." One of his duties was to take a pictorial record of the operation. He had already photographed the ship and most of the activities on the voyage from Honolulu. By the time he had secured his camera case from the cabin, the trawler had hove to, her screws turning over just enough to give steerage control.

"All right," Hartson Brant directed. "Close the hatch."

The boys jumped to help and the heavy steel cover

was lifted into position, the nuts put on, and the wrench hammered firmly to make sure they were tight.

Hartson Brant smiled at his associates. "Well, gentlemen, I think we are ready."

Digger Sears stood by at the winch controls. Two of the seamen held the boom ropes. Rick and Scotty would be responsible for clamping the power cable to the heavy steel Submobile cable, but right now Rick had pictures to take, so Chahda assumed that duty.

Turk Mallane turned the wheel over to the third sailor and joined the group on the afterdeck. "We're 100 feet past the temple," he stated. "In 700 feet of water. Okay?"

Hartson Brant nodded. "Ready? All right, Sears."

The heavy drum turned as Digger gave the winch power. The Submobile lifted from the deck. Rick took a picture, then hastily reset the camera. The Submobile rose above the rail level. At a signal, the seamen hauled the boom ropes. The heavy boom slowly swung, and the Submobile crossed the rail and hung over the water.

The steel cable ran out. The Submobile splashed, then slowly settled beneath the surface. Rick took pictures as fast as he could reset the speed graphic.

"Down," Hartson Brant said. "Fifty feet a minute."

"Fifty feet a minute," Digger repeated.

The steel cable slowly unwound from the big drum, and the creak of the blocks and the cough of the winch engine were the only sounds.

Far below, the Submobile was descending through increasing pressure, into the blackness of the depths. Would it hold up under the enormous weight of water? Or had it already cracked? Was it even now a flattened mass of metal?

Rick peered into the depths and saw nothing but the straight line of cable vanishing into the green water. Near by, Scotty and Chahda methodically fed out electric cable, attaching it to the main cable with patent clamps, otherwise the insulated cable might break of its own weight.

Turk coughed, and the sound was loud.

"Hold at 600 feet," Hartson Brant said.

The cable slowed. "Six hundred feet," Digger droned.

There was a sigh from the assembled watchers.

Hartson Brant looked around and smiled. "Bring it up," he directed, his voice steady. "One hundred feet per minute."

No one spoke as the minutes passed. Then, as the Submobile broke clear of the water and dangled in the air, there was a spontaneous cheer. The observation ports were intact, and there was no sign of water behind the clear quartz.

The sailors pulled on the boom ropes and the Submobile came inboard, to settle on deck without a jar. Instantly the scientists were at work, unscrewing the heavy hatch cover. As they loosened the heavy nuts there was the faint hiss of partially compressed air, then the cover was swung off and Hartson Brant climbed inside.

Rick waited breathlessly until the scientist looked out again. "All intact," he reported, smiling. "One small leak at the aft propeller."

The leak was only a trickle of water, but when the packing plate was loosened, it was found that the enormous pressure had compressed the spun-brass packing into a solid, immovable mass.

"We'll have to clean and repack it," Gordon said ruefully. "No more dives today."

It was an accurate prediction. By the time the shaft had been repacked and resealed, the day was almost gone, and Otera was waiting with supper.

"I think we can plan on four dives a day," Zircon estimated as they ate. "Once we get everything down to a system, that is."

Hartson Brant nodded agreement.

"Who makes the first dive?" Rick wanted to know.

"I know who'd like to," Scotty said, grinning.

Chahda said thoughtfully, "We are three youngs, and three mens, yes? I have a plan. Rick, Scotty, and I draw lots, also Sahibs Brant, Gordon, and Zircon draw."

"A good idea," Hartson Brant agreed. "We all want to make the first dive, and since that's impossible, we'll let chance decide. And now, gentlemen, I suggest that we go ashore and get to bed. We have a busy day before us."

The camp on the peninsula was a cheerful place, the jungle alive with the sounds of birds and insects.

"Evidently the natives haven't been around today," Scotty said. "I wonder why? I'm almost tempted to do a little reconnoitring."

Hartson Brant overruled the suggestion. "Let them come to us, if they will. We'll give them plenty of time before we approach them."

"Wish they come soon," Chahda said. "I have feeling like old Greek they tell me about in school. What is name, please? Man with sword."

"Damocles," Rick remembered. "He had a sword suspended over his head by a thread."

"Is same," Chahda agreed.

"I know what you mean," Scotty nodded. "I feel the

same way, as though we were waiting for something to happen."

"Imagination," Rick scoffed. "Let's hit the hay, kids."

"In broad daylight?" Scotty looked shocked.

"It won't be daylight long," Rick assured him. "And tomorrow is a busy day."

Scotty stifled a yawn. "So was today."

Rick lifted his wrist and looked at the luminous dial of his watch. Half past three! What had awakened him? He lay quietly for a moment, listening. It wasn't a movement. Nothing as tangible as that.

He realized suddenly that he didn't hear the deep, regular breathing that would indicate that Scotty and Chahda slept. His whisper sounded loud. "You guys awake?"

"Something's cooking outside," Scotty whispered. "I don't know what. I can *feel* people around."

A shiver travelled the length of Rick's back. He had felt something malignant in the air, too.

"Not near," Chahda whispered. "In jungle, I think."

As though at a signal, there was the rustle of three mosquito nets as the boys swung out of bed. Rick fumbled for his moccasins and put them on. He heard the rustle of plastic as Scotty slipped his rifle from its case, then the sound of the retractor sliding back, followed by the distinctive *snick* as the bolt rammed home on a cartridge.

Rick kept a seven-cell flashlight under his bed, and Chahda had one of the smaller two-cell kind. With the lights in their hands, ready for use, they tiptoed to the tent flap and looked out. The peninsula was faintly lit by a thin slice of moon, not enough to show

D

them anything. The lap of the waves on the beach was loud.

"Lights," Scotty said.

Rick's powerful beam cut a white swath through the night and lit up the jungle wall. Even his untrained eye could see the movement of foliage.

There was a tiny sound as the safety catch on Scotty's rifle clicked off. "Holy cow!" he exclaimed softly. "There must be a hundred of 'em."

Chahda muttered to himself in soft Hindustani.

"Turn it off," Scotty said.

The darkness flooded in again as the light clicked off. Instantly Rick shivered, his skin crawling as though from the impact of twice a hundred eyes. Then, magically, the feeling was gone, as though a shadow had been withdrawn from the camp.

"They're gone," Scotty said aloud. "What do you suppose they were after?"

Rick heard a noise behind him and whirled, flashlight lifted as a club. The three scientists stood there.

"What's going on?" Hartson Brant demanded.

Rick explained in a few sentences.

"I thought something was wrong," Professor Gordon said.

"I awoke a few moments ago," Zircon added. "I heard Scotty whisper and awoke the others."

"Let's take a look at the jungle," Scotty suggested.

Rick and Chahda brought their lights into play and the party walked to the line of twine that was their safeguard. It looked ridiculous to Rick, but he had to admit that no native had crossed it.

"Maybe this is why we haven't seen them," he suggested.

"I don't think so," Gordon disagreed. "If they wanted to make their presence known, they could come out of the jungle behind it."

Rick's roving light suddenly gleamed on something that hung from a tree just behind the barrier string. "What's that?"

Scotty ducked under and retrieved it. It was a polished leather pouch, held closed by a drawstring. He opened it and Rick shot his light into the interior.

"Let me see that," Gordon demanded. He reached in and produced a bone, a bit of ivory carving, and a piece of dried skin.

"What on earth is that?" Hartson Brant asked.

"I've heard of them," Gordon stated. "But I've never seen one. It's a charm, like the *ouanga* of Haiti, used as a warning." He looked at the faces around him, shadowy in the reflected light. "The snakeskin is a standard symbol of warning. The bone symbolizes human intervention if the warning is ignored. The ivory carving invokes the aid of the ancient gods."

He stowed the odd things in the leather pouch, pulled the drawstring tight.

"My friends," Gordon stated, "we have been warned. I gather that we're not wanted here."

"What do you suggest doing about it?" Hartson Brant asked.

"Nothing," Gordon said decisively. "We're safe unless they cross the tabu, which they haven't dared do. Before they break the tabu they'll have to work themselves up into a great state. We'd know it was coming by the noise. I suggest that we go back to bed."

Mr. Brant and Zircon agreed. Scotty and Chahda had no objection.

As they walked back to their tents, though, Scotty muttered, "That old Greek Damocles was a piker. He had only one sword. From the looks, we have a hundred spears."

"Must you always be so cheerful?" Rick grumbled.

CHAPTER XI

The Dragon God

THE first thing Rick noticed when he came out of his tent in the morning was that the jungle was quiet again. The watchers were back, probably waiting for some reaction to their warning. If so, they were disappointed. The Spindrift party was too anxious to start diving to worry about whether or not their presence was wanted on the island.

Aboard the trawler, Otera had breakfast ready. The Spindrift group, minus Scotty and Gordon, sat down on the hatch to eat. As Rick spooned fresh grapefruit, the other two reappeared, grins on their faces.

"We've been getting ready for our lottery," Gordon announced. Rick saw that he and Scotty carried hats.

"We wrote all our names on scraps of paper," Scotty added. He held up his hat. "Rick, Chahda, and I are in this hat." He held the hat above Zircon's head. "Will you draw one slip, sir?"

Rick stopped breathing. He wanted desperately to make the first dive.

Zircon fumbled around in the inverted hat for a moment, then came up with a folded slip of paper.

Rick watched as the big scientist took his time unfolding it. He squinted at it, held it to the light for a better look, then carefully folded it again. Rick could contain himself no longer. "Who is it?" he pleaded.

Zircon contemplated the slip of paper, then smiled at the eager faces around him.

"The name on the paper," he said, "is . . ." he hesitated, and looked at Chahda. Rick's hopes sank.

"Is Mr. Rick Brant," Zircon continued.

For an instant Rick stared, then he let out a whoop. Scotty and Chahda shook his hand solemnly.

"Now," Gordon said, "let's see which of us goes down with Rick. Chahda, will you draw a slip?" He held out the hat that he carried.

Rick watched as Chahda reached in and produced a folded slip. If only his father's name were chosen . . . but that would be too much luck.

"Mr. Hartson Brant," Chahda read.

And then everyone was congratulating the two Brants on their good fortune while Rick and his father grinned happily, too stunned by such exceptional luck to even talk.

It wasn't until much later that they discovered they had been the victims of a conspiracy. The others of the party, knowing the Brants would never agree to accept the honour of the first dive without taking their chances equally with the rest, had gotten together and worked out a simple plan. All three scraps of paper in Scotty's hat had carried Rick's name. Hartson Brant's name had been written on the three in Gordon's hat.

Hartson Brant finished his coffee and smiled at his son. "All set, Rick?"

"Yes, sir," Rick agreed eagerly. He helped arrange

the oxygen supply, while Zircon and Gordon busied themselves with the salvage cable. Turk Mallane came aft and reported, "We're right over the temple."

"Good," Harston Brant said. "We'll try for the centre of it. Gordon, how's the cable?"

"Ready," Gordon replied.

The salvage cable was wound on a drum controlled by a small winch Gordon had added to the ship's equipment. The thin, strong line of braided steel ran out to the end of the boom, then down to the Submobile where it terminated in a loop, like a steel lasso, that fitted into clamps on the nose. The outer part of the loop fitted into similar clamps on the ends of the extension arms. The size of the loop was automatically controlled by the distance the arms were extended.

Digger Sears took his place at the winch and the seamen manned the boom ropes. Hartson Brant made a final inspection, then motioned Rick to climb in. The boy did so, his heart beating rapidly. He waved at Scotty and Chahda, who were grinning like a couple of Cheshire cats, then moved to the back of the Submobile to make room for his father.

The scientist came in after him and the hatch cover was swung into place. Suddenly there was a deafening clatter as the huge nuts were screwed on and hammered tight. Rick held both hands over his ears.

The clamour stopped and he smiled at his father. Hartson Brant smiled back. "Change places with me, Rick. If you're going to be a scientist, you might as well start learning to handle delicate equipment."

"Yes, sir!" Rick exclaimed. "Thanks, Dad." He had never expected to handle the Sonoscope and the salvage equipment in an actual dive, even though he had been careful to learn about their operation. He moved to the front of the Submobile and took a seat on the metal bench. Hartson Brant went to the aft position where he would watch the oxygen-supply rate, handle the telephone—which was a mouthpiece-earphone unit like that of a telephone operator—and control the three propellers.

The Submobile deck was level, all the electric motors hidden under it. The front panel that Rick faced was like a flat, steel wall, separating the operator from the equipment within the nose.

On the right upper portion of the panel was a ground-glass screen, eight inches long and six wide. It was dark now, because the Sonoscope had not been turned on. Below the screen were four controls that turned on the instrument, controlled the amount of power fed into it, and focused it. Directly above it was an illuminated scale that showed the distance of the Sonoscope's target in feet.

The Sonoscope sound transmitter on the nose sent out bursts of supersonic waves, many vibrations per second above the range a human ear could hear. These bursts of sound would strike an object and reflect. This echo would be picked up and translated into electronic impulses. Since the time of the echo would vary, according to the distance of the various parts of the object, the electronic impulses would also vary in strength. Using the electronic impulses to operate a cathode tube and projecting them on the screen, which was actually the wide part of the tube, would give a picture of the object on which the Sonoscope was trained.

To the left of the Sonoscope the wall was cut away to give vision through the forward observation port, a square piece of fused quartz about five inches thick.

Under the observation port were two pairs of pistol grips. The triggers were motor switches, and buttons under the thumbs of the operator controlled various functions of the salvage equipment. The pistol grips moved in a circle, controlling the direction of the equipment in use. One pair of grips operated the extension arms, the other pair the salvage scoop.

Rick looked up at the bank of instruments at the top of the panel. One told him that the Submobile was receiving normal electrical voltage. Others would show him the frequency of the Sonoscope impulses, inner and outer temperatures, and similar information.

He hurriedly put on his own pair of earphones as the Submobile lifted from the deck. He caught a glimpse of the trawler's deck through the observation port as they swung out over the water, then they splashed gently into the sea and green water foamed up past the quartz opening.

"Turn on the searchlight," Hartson Brant suggested. "You might see some fish."

Rick snapped the proper switch on the switch panel to his right, but the water was still too sunlit to see the beam.

"Everything all right, Gordon," Hartson Brant said.

"Right," Gordon replied in the earphones. "We're taking you down to 580."

Rick saw the keel of the *Tarpon* overhead and the growth of green stuff on her hull. He saw the screws turning over slowly as the ship held position, then the trawler's keel seemed to slide upward through the green water and vanish from sight.

A brightly coloured little fish about two inches long peered through the port with goggle eyes, then disappeared with a flick of a fanlike tail. A brown shape passed, just out of range of his vision, but Rick couldn't guess what it was. A shark or a porpoise, probably.

"One hundred feet," Gordon said in the earphones.

The green colour had deepened to blue, and now all trace of green vanished. The searchlight cut a yellow, sharply defined path through the blue water. Rick sat spellbound, eagerly watching for signs of life outside the observation port. Now and then he saw fish at a distance too great for identification, and once a long, almost transparent ribbon swam into the searchlight beam and out again.

As the Submobile sank deeper, he began to see flickers of light outside the beam.

"Some sort of undersea life," Mr. Brant explained. "At this depth, many forms carry their own lights."

A cloud of tiny objects the size of hazelnuts drifted past, and the scientist identified them as jellyfish. "Thimble jellies," he said. "So called because of their size and shape."

The blue colour was darker now, but it was still amazingly bright. It was deceptive, because when Rick looked at his instruments, he couldn't make them out at all and had to turn on the panel lights.

A fish that seemed to be mostly head and jaws went past, and as it passed out of the searchlight beam, Rick saw rows of luminous dots along its side. His father called it "a hatchet fish, very common at this depth."

Suddenly Rick felt as though an invisible hand had pushed him toward the bottom of the Submobile. He realized that their descent had stopped, causing the elevatorlike feeling. At the same moment, Gordon spoke in the earphones. They were at 580 feet.

"Turn on the Sonoscope," Hartson Brant directed.

Rick turned the proper knob and the ground-glass screen glowed a fitful green. He turned the focus knobs, but nothing showed. A glance at the instruments told him the Sonoscope was sending out its inaudible bursts of sound at 50,000 vibrations per second, far above the range of the human ear, which can hear only up to about 20,000 cycles per second.

"Take us down five feet," the scientist ordered into his mouthpiece.

Rick bent over the Sonoscope screen. Little by little a picture swam up from the bottom of the glowing green glass. He looked at the image of massive blocks, sketched in varying shades of luminous green.

"I have something, Dad."

Hartson Brant looked over his shoulder. "Yes. We're inside the temple wall. That must be the remnants of some sort of building."

Rick brought the image into sharper focus, and exclaimed, "Look at the steps!" They were clearly defined —a low, broad flight that had once led to what might have been the temple itself. Rick could almost picture warriors in crested helmets walking up those steps while priests chanted and incense swirled around the faces of forgotten gods.

The Submobile swayed slightly on its cable, and on the left side of the screen something flickered briefly before the undersea craft swung back again.

"There was something there," Rick said excitedly. "Can we swing around, Dad?"

For answer, Hartson Brant threw his switches and the drone of motors made the floor vibrate. He moved a control and the starboard propeller turned, swinging the Submobile around.

Rick turned the focus knobs as the thing he had glimpsed moved to the centre of the screen. At last it glowed bright, in sharp focus. He stared in disbelief, and his mouth opened.

"Holy leaping snakes," he shouted. "It's a sea serpent!"

CHAPTER XII

Worshippers of the Bronze God

HARTSON BRANT moved quickly and looked over Rick's shoulder. The object on the screen had a long, sinuous body terminating in a gross, misshapen head that seemed part alligator, part lion, and part snake. Wings sprouted from between humped shoulders, and thick legs seemed to grope for the bottom.

"Not a sea serpent," Hartson Brant said. "Something even more valuable!" He spoke into the phone. "Gordon! We have something on the screen. See if the salvage cable is free."

In a moment the Submobile swayed slightly and Gordon answered, his voice excited. "It's free. What do you have?"

"Statuary of some sort," Mr. Brant answered. "We'll try for it."

"You'd better take over, Dad," Rick said, starting to move.

"Nonsense. You can snare it, Rick. Go to it."

Rick wiped moist palms on his thighs and swallowed. He leaned over and looked through the observation port, but the searchlights showed nothing.

"We'll have to get closer," he said. "The Sonoscope

109

scale shows thirty feet and I can't see anything through the port."

The scientist gave power to the aft propeller motor and the Submobile moved slowly ahead. Rick left his seat and knelt before the observation port, his eyes trying to pierce the gloom. Little by little the thing took form, a dark shape in the yellow gleam of the search-light. It was hard to judge the size, but he thought it was about eight feet long, from the open jaws to the long tail, and it sat on a base just big enough for the four legs.

Rick took the pistol grips in his hands and squeezed the triggers. The motors under the deck responded and he heard the whine of gears ahead of the instrument panel. Now he had to drop the loop of the cable over the sea beast's head. He worked slowly, with frequent pauses to look through the observation port. Pulling down on the grips elevated the arms. He let them carry the cable past the head, the left arm over the thing's back, the right one in the air well ahead of the nose.

He dropped the left arm on the statue's back and left it there, then he dropped the right arm past the nose and pulled it in against the scaly chest.

The cable now ran from the Submobile out along the left arm, across the statue's back and down past the neck to the other arm against the chest. Working care-fully, he retracted the right arm fully. Then, with equal care, he retracted the left arm, and he could feel the cable catch! It passed across the statue's back, and returned under the thing's head. He had it hooked! He brought the left arm back into rest position, and turned to his father, grinning with such pleased relief that his face hurt.

"Got it, Dad!"

"Nice going, son." Hartson Brant mopped his perspiring face. "I was working as hard as you were, just watching. Okay, Rick. Drop the cable."

Rick pulled the release knobs and the cable dropped from the grips, free of the Submobile.

"We have it, John," Hartson Brant said into the mouthpiece. "Take up the slack, but very slowly."

The scientist gunned the motors and the Submobile moved a few degrees. Dimly, with the aid of the searchlight, they saw the noose of the cable slowly tighten around the statue's neck. It stirred, raising a murky cloud that blotted out the view.

"Take us up," Mr. Brant ordered.

Rick switched off the Sonoscope and sat back. Mr. Brant cut the propeller motor switches and there was silence in the Submobile.

The ascent seemed to take much longer than the downward trip, but Rick knew it was only his eagerness to see what they had captured. At last the blue of the water turned to green, and finally they broke clear into sunlight that made him blink. They were swung to the deck and again there was the terrific clanging as the hatch was removed.

They jumped to the deck to greet curious faces.

"What is it?" Scotty asked excitedly.

"A real sea monster," Rick answered. He hurried to the rail and looked down to where the salvage cable vanished into the depths. "Can we bring it up right away?" he asked.

"We're going to." Hartson Brant smiled. "Captain, will you bring it up? Slowly, please. If it's soft stone, we don't want to break it."

Turk nodded. "Easy does it." He threw the switch and the electric winch began to turn. "Not much weight on it. It can't be very heavy."

Digger Sears watched from the pilothouse door. Otera peered from the galley. Even the two sailors, who were doing nothing at the moment, lost some of their usual impassiveness and watched over the rail.

Presently Chahda shouted, "Is coming!"

A dark bulk appeared, far down in the water. It came into sight, a weird monster eight feet long and about four feet high, not counting the upflung wings.

"My sainted aunt," Scotty gasped. "It is a sea monster!"

The statue broke water and dangled at the end of the cable amid excited gasps from the watchers. It was a dragon! The broad, alligator jaws were open, showing jagged teeth and a forked tongue. Snakelike scales covered it, extending down the front legs to webbed feet that gripped a flat base. But the rear portion was like the hindquarters of a lion, or a great cat, except for the tail. Rick couldn't imagine what the tail represented. It was thick and tapering, and it had a row of spines along its top.

The sailors swung the boom in and held the dripping object just above the rail. Gordon was examining it instantly. He opened his jack-knife and scraped, and bright metal showed though the scratch.

"Bronze!" he exclaimed. "Rick, you're a wonder! Remind me to make you a vice-president or something. We must get it ashore at once. I want to clean and examine it."

"Of course," Hartson Brant said. "It will fit in the whaleboat without trouble. Captain, how much does it weigh?"

"About 500 pounds," Turk replied. "Maybe a little more. The whaleboat will take it." He ordered the seamen to bring the boat alongside. The centre seat was removed and the statue lowered. Professor Gordon, Hartson Brant, and one of the seamen got in and the salvage noose was loosened and hauled out of the way.

"Rick!" Hartson Brant called. "Fix up a block and tackle. We'll need it to get this thing ashore."

Rick ran to obey as the boat cast off and headed for shore. The trawler swung around and followed it through the reef pass, anchoring close to shore. Then Turk and Digger Sears joined Rick and the others in the second small boat.

Gordon was already at work with his cleaning tools, removing the accumulated covering of centuries. He was reluctant to stop even to get the statue into a working place on land.

Under Hartson Brant's direction, Rick, Scotty, and Chahda took axes and a machete and cut down three young trees at the jungle's edge. They were about four inches thick and fifteen feet long when trimmed and cut to even lengths. They were lashed together about two feet from the top, and set up in the form of a pyramid, the block and tackle secured to the junction point.

The tackle was quickly secured to the statue, then willing hands tugged on the rope while the others guided the unwieldy thing. It swung out of the boat and came to rest under the pyramid of poles.

Professor Gordon suddenly exclaimed, "Wait a moment, I have an idea!"

He found a tape measure and quickly measured the statue's base; then he hurried to the stone rectangle and measured its top. "Just as I thought," he said happily. "A perfect fit. It's just the right height for working, too. Can we get it up there?"

"Easily," Hartson Brant assured him.

The pyramid of poles was moved toward the stone pedestal, and the statue pulled closer. By moving the poles and the block and tackle several times, the statue was finally moved next to the stone. One more adjustment of the poles and it was lifted and dropped into place. As Gordon had said, it was a perfect fit.

"Some gadget," Scotty said admiringly.

The statue was a strange-looking object. Half animal, half reptile, it seemed to crouch, jaws extended.

Chahda suddenly turned and looked at the jungle. "You hear what I hear?" he demanded.

Scotty had turned, too. "Sounded like one of the natives got a good look and it scared him silly. He took off on the run."

"I heard something," Rick agreed. It had sounded like a man crashing through the underbrush. "Maybe we've got a better tabu gimmick than the pieces of handkerchief," he said.

Gordon was working on the statue, removing the coating of grime and scale. Rick found a can of gasoline and helped out with a rag dipped in the gas. It acted as a solvent, removing the last traces of the outer coating. Little by little, the dragon god began to shine in all his bronze glory—or ugliness.

As they finished working on the muscular legs, Scotty said, "Company's come. Lots of them this time."

Rick looked toward the jungle and thought he saw movement in the dense foliage. "Let's give 'em a good look at our new pal," he suggested.

He, Chahda, Gordon, and big Hobart Zircon had been standing in front of the statue. They moved back, exposing it to the view of the watchers in the jungle.

A huge wave of sound swelled from the woods, a mass sigh, mixed with groans. The foliage crackled as bodies pushed through it.

Scotty jumped for his rifle.

Rick gasped. Natives! More than a hundred of them! And they were all flat on their faces just behind the tabu line, outstretched in worship of the dragon god on the pedestal!

"Get Otera," Hartson Brant told Chahda. "Perhaps he can speak their language."

As though at a signal, the natives rose and stood looking across the barrier at the white men.

Rick looked at them curiously. They were tall, on the average, with good features and brown skins. They wore the skirtlike garment of the ancient Pacific people. They were muscular and clean looking, but their faces were not pleasant.

"A tough bunch of monkeys," Scotty whispered. "What are they? Polynesians or Mongols?"

It was a fair question, since many of them had the Mongoloid eye fold that gives the look of slant eyes.

"A little of both," Gordon answered. He walked toward the silent, watching throng. "What name you come 'long dis fella place?"

The line of natives stirred, but there was no answer. Minutes ticked away as the two groups faced each other, watching silently. Then an old man stepped right up to the tabu string. He held out both hands expressively and shrugged.

"He doesn't understand," Rick said. He turned and looked toward the trawler. Otera was on his way in the whaleboat with Chahda.

"These gooks never understand," Turk Mallane said. "Only when they think it will get them something."

"Too ruddy right," Digger Sears agreed. "Give 'em a fistful o' smokes and watch the blokes come to life."

The boat grounded and Chahda and Otera ran to join the party. At Gordon's instructions, Otera walked toward the line of natives, a little fearfully. He jabbered a few words in a language that seemed to consist entirely of vowels.

The old chief's face lit up. He replied rapidly in the same language.

"Dis one fella chief," Otera told Gordon.

Rick strained to follow the rapid patter of *bêché-de-mer*, but got lost. Gordon translated when Otera had finished talking.

"This is evidently the Number One chief, and all the males of the tribe. He says that the dragon god is the ancient god of his people. It was swallowed by the sea many years before the time of the oldest of his ancestors. Once they had a small one they made, but it was broken. Now the original god has been returned to them, and they wish us to lift the tabu, so they may worship."

Gordon had a queer look on his face. "He adds something about our profaning the place. He wants us to get out."

Hartson Brant considered. "Have Otera point out that without us the dragon god wouldn't have been restored. We'll lift the tabu for them, but only for a while. Make that clear."

"Profaning the place, eh?" Turk grunted. "I'll profane 'em with the toe of my boot."

Rick went with Sooty and Gordon to remove the twine with its burden of handkerchief strips. He noticed that Scotty carried his rifle.

He helped gather in the string, very conscious of the row of natives only a few feet away. Once he stopped to look at them more closely, and fierce eyes met his.

They stood aside to let the natives pass, but, surprisingly, the warriors melted into the jungle.

"What the heck!" Scotty exclaimed. "I hope they haven't gone for their bows and arrows."

"You and me," Rick agreed wholeheartedly. "They're a rough-looking crowd."

"Here they come again," Gordon said. The three hurried back to where the others had gathered near the statue.

The natives had evidently gone into the jungle to pick up their dearest possessions from wherever they had stored them. They returned, carrying carved war clubs, strings of cowrie shells, great bunches of young coconuts and bananas. There were delicately carved combs and bowls, and ludicrous things like bits of broken alarm clock, rusted tobacco tins, and other salvage.

These offerings were piled before the dragon god while the old chief watched; then the natives gathered in a semicircle, looking at the fierce thing, their eyes worshipful.

Turk Mallane laughed heartily. "That's the way to make points with your own special heaven," he said. "Offer a hunk of alarm clock as a sacrifice."

A hundred pair of eyes turned to him.

"Keep quiet," Hartson Brant ordered. He turned to Rick and Scotty. "Break out some of those canned rations in our tent. We'll see if we can't make friends."

Rick and Scotty ran to the scientists' tent and found a case of rations. They carried it back and tore the cardboard cover off, then waited for instructions.

Hartson Brant motioned to them to remain quiet. The chief had started a ceremonial chanting before the dragon god. Then the warriors joined in and the throbbing chant increased in volume.

It was strangely stirring, even though Rick couldn't guess what they were chanting. Unconsciously he began to sway with the rhythm of the chant, and, like the warriors, his eyes were focused on the weird bronze statue. Then, abruptly, the chant ended, on a high, wailing note, and the warriors stirred and began looking around them at the camp.

"Now," Hartson Brant said.

Rick took a handful of cans from the ration crates and offered them to the nearest warriors. They looked at the shiny tins, not understanding.

"Open one," Chahda suggested.

Rick signed for the warriors to watch. He took the can key and unwound the metal strip that sealed it. Then he lifted out the compressed beef in it, took his jack-knife, cut off a slice and ate it.

The nearest warrior, a husky young man who towered over Rick, watched suspiciously. When Rick held out the beef he sniffed at it like a suspicious hound, then reached for the shining can. Rick held the can away from him and offered the beef again. With a frown the young warrior accepted it, lifted it and sank strong white teeth into the mixture.

There was silence as he chewed. The other natives had gathered, watching. Then the young warrior's face cleared and he nodded. He held out his hand for more.

It was a signal for the other natives to crowd around the ration box. Scotty, aided by Chahda and Zircon, laughingly motioned them back while the cans were opened. The contents had to be divided or some of the natives would be left out. One whole can, however, went to the old chief, along with a sheath knife from the camping kit.

Rick grinned, watching the press of natives anxious to taste canned food. They were crowding around and laughing like children.

Then, from the centre of the milling crowd, there was a sudden yell of anger and the sound of a hard blow as fist met flesh. The laughter stilled and the natives stepped back.

The old chief was stretched on the ground, just stirring back to consciousness, and over him Digger Sears stood nursing his knuckles.

The mate looked belligerently around him. "The old gook tried to pick me pocket!" he explained angrily.

"A bunch of thieves," Turk Mallane agreed. "I knew you'd have trouble."

Rick looked at the captain in amazement. He was calmly eating a banana filched from the sacrificial pile!

"Put those bananas back," Hartson Brant ordered coldly. "Sears, get back to the ship and don't come ashore again."

Scotty was already helping the old chief to his feet. The ageing warrior pulled away proudly and walked into the jungle without looking back.

"Go ahead," Turk said disdainfully. "Pamper the

swine. Let 'em worship old Joe Goblin. They'll steal your shirts while you're doing it.'' He slapped the bronze statue casually.

There was an angry mutter from the native warriors.

"I don't like this,'' Professor Gordon whispered to Rick. "I think we'd better get the tabu back up. He motioned to Otera and told him what to say.

The natives looked at Otera as he talked, then, without a word, they walked back into the jungle. Rick and Gordon hurried after them and hastily strung the tabu line once more.

"I don't like it,'' Gordon said again. "Between them, Turk and Digger did just about everything possible to prevent friendly relations.''

They returned in time to hear the finish of what Hartson Brant had to say to Turk Mallane.

"... and I'd prefer that you and your crew remain aboard the ship in the future, Captain. That is an order.''

Turk's face was brick red, but he accepted it. "All right. If brotherly love with a pack of natives is what you want, we'll not interfere.'' He stalked down to the shore and got into the boat where Digger was waiting.

"Your dad really told Turk off,'' Scotty said as he and Rick took the empty ration box and the cans to the junk pile.

Chahda joined them, his face serious. "Plenty no good, what Turk and Digger do. You think we make friends with the natives now?''

"Not a chance,'' Scotty said decisively.

"You're right,'' Rick agreed. "They've had their pride hurt, and they look to me like a pretty proud bunch. We'll be lucky if we don't have trouble with them.'' He looked at the thin twine with its strips of handkerchief. "We're putting a lot of faith in a hunk of string and some rags."

Scotty glanced at the tabu line. "My faith in that thing isn't what it used to be," he admitted.

CHAPTER XIII

Trapped

THE cable was running out from the main winch, lowering the Submobile for its first dive of the morning, when Scotty told Rick what had been on his mind.

"I'm getting uneasy about leaving the camp. The natives were watching this morning. There wasn't a sound in the jungle."

"I noticed that." Rick put a clamp on the power line and secured it to the cable. "Do you think they'll break the tabu?"

Chadha joined them in time to hear Rick's question. "I think maybe yes," he said. "Before, they would not. But now the dragon god is behind the tabu, and they want the dragon god."

"That's what I think," Scotty agreed. "And there's something else we've kind of forgotten. How about our friend in the paint locker?"

"I haven't forgotten him," Rick denied. "But what can we do about him? Turk keeps him locked up, except for a while in the morning before we start diving and again at night when we're through."

"Is spooky business," Chahda mused. "I get creeps in my bones."

Zircon interrupted, calling an order to Digger Sears at the winch control. "Give them another five feet. They have something on the Sonoscope screen."

"Another dragon?" Rick asked eagerly.

"Your father thinks it's the inner wall of the temple," the big scientist replied. "They're going to pry a piece loose with the scoop, if they can."

The boys waited, watching Zircon. Once the tone of the generator deepened and the cable moved a few inches. Down below, the Submobile would be jockeying for a better position.

"They have it!" Zircon boomed exultantly. "All right, Sears. Bring them up, but slowly."

As the Submobile came up through the water Rick could make out a heavy slab of stone firmly locked between the jaws of the scoop. The stone was covered with what looked like a cross between Chinese picture writing and hieroglyphics.

It was a jubilant pair of scientists that climbed out of the Submobile. "We found the temple itself," Hartson Brant said. "It seems to be almost intact. With any luck, we should be able to bring up most of it."

Professor Gordon had already hurried to the stone slab. "This is more than I had hoped for," he exclaimed. "If we can translate it, we may find some of the answers archaeologists have been seeking for years. Hartson, I'd like to get this ashore at once."

Turk Mallane had come out of the pilothouse to see what the Submobile had brought up. "Sure," he said. "Here, I'll give you a hand and we can put it into one of the small boats."

In a moment, with one of the sailors helping, the slab

was safely stowed. Gordon looked around. "I'd like someone to help me ashore. Who wants to go?"

"I go," Chahda said quickly. He climbed into the boat and took the oars. In a moment he and Gordon were on their way to camp.

Turk stopped to speak to Rick and Scotty. "We've been lucky," he said. "Even the weather has been on our side, but it's not going to hold much longer."

Rick looked at the cloudless sky. "Not much sign of bad weather now."

"I know this part of the world," Turk said. "Three days without rain is a long time." He went back to the pilothouse.

Scotty stared after him. "We," he said. "He talks as though he had a half share in the expedition."

"He's been pretty good about co-operating," Rick pointed out. "I don't like him much, because he blows hot and cold on alternate days. He can't decide whether he wants to be a grouch or a good guy. But he's been a lot of help."

"Sure," Scotty said. "Come on, let's help check the Submobile."

Hobart Zircon asked, "Want to go down with me, Scotty?"

Scotty definitely did and said so with enthusiasm. He and the scientist got into the Submobile and Rick and Hartson Brant tightened down the hatch. As they were finishing, Turk came out of the pilothouse.

"I'll give you a hand back here," he offered. "The helmsman can keep the ship steady without me."

"Are you sure?" Rick asked doubtfully.

"He's a good man," Turk replied. "Don't worry."

The second dive was as successful as the first. A few

moments after they reached 590 feet, Scotty phoned up that they had a second piece of the temple slab. It proved to be smaller than the first one, but bore even more interesting carvings depicting helmeted warriors going into battle. Even through the layer of dirt Rick could see that the warriors had regular features. Their helmets were like those of ancient Greece.

Hartson Brant was excited over the find. "Gordon must see this right away," he exclaimed. "Captain, will you have one of the men row me to camp?"

Turk motioned to one of the seamen. "Take Mr. Brant ashore, but come right back." To the others, he explained with a grin, "I don't like to have both of my lifeboats away at once. You never know when you'll need one."

Zircon looked around as the boat departed. "Our little group is depleted," he said. "Do you suppose that could mean a double ration of lunch for us? Or has everyone but me forgotten that it is lunchtime?"

"You took the words right out of my mouth," Scotty approved. "Let's see what Otera has for us."

Otera had a fresh salad, sandwiches, and a cold, fruit drink. Turk joined them at lunch on the hatch, and gestured toward the camp. "That's the trouble with scientific enthusiasm. It makes you forget your meals."

"There's another case of rations ashore," Scotty told him. "They can manage."

Turk seemed inclined to talk. "How long do you think we'll be at this?" he asked Zircon.

The scientist shrugged. "That's hard to say. Why do you ask?"

"I'd surely like to make one dive before we go back," Turk said.

"Of course," Zircon boomed. "The only professional among us and you haven't been down yet. Unless we get further instructions from Hartson, why not go down this afternoon?"

"I'd appreciate the chance," Turk said eagerly.

Rick didn't quite know why he felt disapproval. "Will you go down with him, sir?" he asked Zircon.

The big scientist thought it over. "No," he said finally. "I think one of us older folks should be on deck at all times. No offence, boys. I'm sure you understand. You may go down with the captain, Rick."

It would have been pointless to refuse. Rick nodded.

After lunch, the usual check of the Submobile was made. The sailor who had taken Hartson Brant ashore had returned, and Otera could lend a hand with the boom ropes, so there would be no shortage of help.

Rick climbed in followed by Turk, and the hatch swung closed behind them. In a moment they were settled, the phone circuit checked, and the order was given to swing them over the side.

Rick would have liked to watch out the forward observation port as they went down, but Turk gave him no chance. The captain was full of questions. He wanted to know everything about the operation of the Submobile. He listened eagerly to Rick's explanations and made him repeat everything to be sure he had it straight.

It was natural enough, Rick thought. After all, Turk was a professional salvage man.

They hardly noticed the Submobile descent until Zircon called that they were at 585 feet. Rick turned on the Sonoscope and focused it with Turk watching over his shoulder. The screen glowed with the green image of stairs, ending in what seemed to be a carved door.

Rick snapped on the searchlight and looked through the observation port. The light, an intense yellow at this depth, showed him the stairs, ending in the wall of the temple. A row of carvings on the wall had split away in some places. Evidently an ancient craftsman had carved his picture stories on thin squares of stone that were later cemented to the wall.

"I think we can get one of those," Rick said. He gauged the distance, pausing to watch a deep-sea eel swim into the light and out again.

Turk's black eyes were shining. "How do we do it? With the salvage arms or the scoop?"

"The scoop," Rick answered. "The salvage arms are only for things big enough to slip a noose around, although they can be used to handle drills, or to set charges. We'll have to get closer, Turk."

"Here we go," Turk said. He moved back and turned on the propeller motors. Rick watched to be sure he was doing it properly. Then Turk took the aft propeller control and moved it carefully. The Submobile swayed a little and drifted closer to the temple wall. Turk retarded the control, working with it until the propeller was turning just enough to hold them in position with the scoop within easy reach of the wall.

Rick nodded. Turk had the touch, all right.

The captain grinned. "Easy as pie. Running this thing is a cinch."

"It's supposed to be," Rick told him. "Dad and the others always plan a thing so that the controls will be simple enough for an untrained operator. Now, let's go after that nearest slab."

"How about letting me operate the scoop?" Turk asked.

"Okay." Rick changed places with him.

Turk had the telephone mouthpiece slung around his neck and he kept it on as he moved into the forward operating position. He spoke to the deck. "We're going after a piece of slab on the temple wall."

Rick heard Zircon's reply in his own earphones. "Right. All okay on deck."

Turk took the pistol grips that controlled the salvage scoop and tried swinging it in order to get the feel of the controls. Then, watching the Sonoscope, he went after the slab. Once he paused and refocused the image on the screen. After the briefest of tries, the scoop jaws locked firmly on the slab.

"Got it!" he exclaimed. "Lad, this is the greatest machine I've ever seen. It will revolutionize diving."

Rick nodded. "You operate the thing like a veteran, Turk."

"Nothing to it," Turk returned. He spoke into the mouthpiece. "Hello on deck. All quiet?"

"All quiet," Zircon returned.

"Let me talk with Digger Sears, will you?"

Rick looked at the captain in surprise.

In a moment the mate's voice came down the wire. "Aye, Turk?"

"Easy to operate as a hand shovel, Digger. How's it look on deck?"

"Good-O."

"Then get to it."

"Righto."

The phone went dead.

"What was that about?" Rick demanded.

"Keep your shirt on," Turk said. "Shut those propeller motors off and let's get clear for surfacing."

Rick did so, a sudden apprehension forming within him. The feeling grew as the minutes passed and they did not move from the bottom. "What's going on?" he asked. "Why are we sitting down here like this?"

Turk reached into his hip pocket and came out with a leather blackjack. He slapped it into the palm of his hand, his eyes on Rick.

"We'll be going up as soon as your friends are taken care of."

Rick's heart jumped into his mouth. "Taken care of!"

"Oh, nothing serious," Turk assured him, smiling, "unless they put up too much of a struggle."

Rick leaned back against the wall and stared at the captain. He had a mental picture of Scotty and Zircon facing the entire crew, and maybe the Japanese stowaway!

"You've been waiting for a chance like this!" he burst out. "You waited until the party was split up. . . ."

"And until I had made a dive with a good teacher," Turk finished.

"But why?" Rick asked hoarsely. He gauged the distance, and his legs drew up under him.

Turk leaned forward, his eyes hard. "Don't try anything, kid. I'll slug you if you give me half an excuse."

Rick subsided, knowing that he didn't have a chance.

"Tough lines," Turk said. "We're taking over, as of now. But we won't be diving for the temple. We're after big game!"

The words formed without thinking. "The ship on the bottom!" Of course! Why hadn't he realized it all along?

E

"Yes," Turk agreed. "That's the *Asamo* over yonder. You never heard of her, I take it. Few have. Sit quietly and give me no trouble and I'll tell you about it."

Rick nodded. There was nothing else he could do. He was in an agony of worry for Scotty and Professor Zircon, but he couldn't help them, trapped as he was with Turk Mallane in almost a hundred fathoms of water.

It was a strange tale that Turk told, starting in the first year of the war against Japan. In the first months of the war, the Japanese had overrun a great part of south-eastern Asia, and they had rifled Singapore, the Dutch Indies, Rabaul, Manila, Hong Kong, and other places of vast amounts of valuables. The cruiser *Asamo* had been sent to collect the smaller, more valuable stuff and to take it to Japan.

Netherlands Intelligence, through espionage agents in the Indies, had learned of the plan, and the *Asamo's* route. A Dutch submarine, based at Perth, Australia, had been given orders to intercept the cruiser. The interception had taken place off Kwangara, and a torpedo had crippled the *Asamo* and sent her running for cover. A second torpedo caught her just off the tip of Little Kwangara and she had gone to the bottom.

Turk's black eyes gleamed. "We don't even know how much treasure she has, except that it's counted in the millions. Gems, pearls, gold bullion, plate, even cash money. There's more than a million just in pearls. We know they got that much when the Japs butchered the Australian garrison at Rabaul."

Digger Sears spoke through the earphones. "All dinkum, Turk. We're bringin' you topside."

"Much trouble?" Turk asked casually.

Rick's heart stopped while he waited for the reply.

"Not much. Otera took a hand and we had to clip him. The others are in the galley. Hash is guardin' 'em."

Digger rang off, and in a moment the Submobile stirred and started its voyage upward.

"Hash is Soyu Hashimo," Turk explained for Rick's benefit. "He was an officer on the *Asamo*. He and Digger got together while Hash was in an Aussie prison camp. When the war ended, he sneaked Hash away and brought him to me. Wasn't much I could do about it, on account of the *Asamo* being below diving depth. Then I read a yarn in the papers about this expedition, and I saw the ad for a skipper."

"The perfect answer, wasn't it?" Rick said bitterly.

"Perfect," Turk agreed. "If you'd been a little smarter, you could have added two and two. You almost caught Hash when he came to see me at the hotel. You saw him on the dock."

"No wonder you co-operated," Rick said. "You wanted the dives to go off smoothly while you watched and learned how the equipment operated. You were so friendly you made me sick."

Turk chuckled. He was in high good humour, but his black eyes never left Rick and the blackjack was held ready for use.

Rick closed his eyes. It was his fault. Hadn't he had warning that something was afoot? But Turk's co-operative friendliness had lulled him into a false security. Why hadn't they kept better guard?

"You can't get away with it," he stated finally. "When the expedition fails to return on schedule, Dr. Warren will have the Navy look for us."

"They'll find us," Turk said. "But they won't find you. And why? You'll be on Kwangara, my boy."

The Submobile broke clear of the water and swung inboard to settle lightly on the deck. Turk took a firmer grip on the blackjack. "Don't be foolish enough to try anything."

"I won't," Rick said dully. He knew he didn't have a chance.

The hatch swung open and Digger's grinning face looked in.

"Out you go," Turk ordered.

Rick climbed to the deck and looked around. There was no sign of his friends, but the Japanese was standing in the galley door—and he was holding Scotty's rifle!

He submitted while one of the sailors lashed his hands behind him, then Digger shoved him toward the galley. Rick almost fell over something that looked like a heavy pipe set in a metal plate. It was held upright by two legs.

"Keep movin'," Digger snapped and gave Rick another push. The Jap stepped aside as he went headlong through the galley door.

Scotty and Zircon looked up at him. Otera was huddled in a corner, his bushy hair dark with blood.

"What happened?" Rick asked despairingly. He saw that Scotty had a welt over one eye.

"We had no warning," Zircon said heavily. "Digger Sears handed me the phone, and while I was putting the mouthpiece around my neck, he thrust a pistol into my ribs."

"I made a jump for my rifle," Scotty said. "One of the sailors threw a wrench. It caught me a glancing blow over the eye. By the time I got back to my feet, he was covering me with my own gun."

"Otera came running out of the galley with a knife," Zircon continued. "The sailor in the pilothouse stepped out behind him and struck him with a length of pipe. He hasn't stirred since."

The sudden throb of the Diesel engines told them that the trawler was under way.

Rick explained briefly what Turk had told him.

"So that's it," Scotty said. "I saw the mortar. They have shells, too. But what do they intend doing with it?"

"We'll know shortly," Zircon said.

The Japanese looked in at them and spoke in perfect English. "Make no noise, my friends, or I'll be forced to shoot."

"Stand outside, you yellow ape," Scotty growled. "We don't want to look at you."

The Japanese walked over to the bound boy and deliberately kicked him in the ribs.

Scotty turned white, but he made no sound.

"You'll be sorry for that," Rick stated hotly.

Turk appeared in the doorway just as the anchor chain rattled out. "On your feet."

Out on deck, Digger had opened a box and was taking out what looked like miniature bombs. Turk pointed to them. "You see those? One peep out of any of you and we'll drop a few among your friends on shore. We're untying your hands, but I'll be right behind you with this." He held up a pistol.

They were herded into the boat under Turk's watchful eyes. He had been careful to bring the boat to the side of the trawler away from the camp. The people ashore couldn't see what was going on.

Two sailors brought Otera out and placed him in the bottom of the boat, then Turk's pistol urged Scotty,

Zircon, and Rick into the boat. Turk motioned to the sailors. "Row, you two."

Turk had planned well. As the boat rounded the trawler, Hartson Brant, Professor Gordon, and Chahda waved and walked down to the beach to meet them. Before they realized anything was wrong, they were covered by Turk's pistol.

The two sailors ran past the astonished scientists and began to search the camp methodically. Hartson Brant, Gordon, and Chahda asked questions and were ordered to be still. The Spindrift party stood silently until the sailors finished and reported no weapons in camp.

"All right," Turk said. "Stand quietly, all of you. Digger has orders to drop a couple of mortar shells around your ears if you make any funny moves." He backed to the nearest boat and got in, followed by a sailor. The other took the second boat. In a moment they were headed back to the ship while the boys and the scientists watched helplessly. Then Gordon dropped to his knees beside Otera and lifted the cook's wrist.

"His pulse is strong," he said. "Rick, get the first-aid kit."

While Gordon bandaged Otera, the three who had been aboard ship told their stories.

"Now we have answers to many questions," Chahda said. "But it do us no goods."

"No," Hartson Brant agreed. "No good at all."

Rick sat down on the ground and stared out to the trawler. They were in a bad spot, trapped on a tiny spit of land with Turk and his crew in front of them, and, behind them, a jungle that was ominously silent.

CHAPTER XIV

Mutiny Aboard the "Tarpon"

RICK went into the dark tent and bent over Otera. The cook was sleeping quietly. Rick tucked in the mosquito netting again, then looked over at Scotty's bunk. He was sound asleep, his face peaceful in the reflected glow of the flashlight.

Outside the tent, Chahda was sitting, wrapped in his blanket because the night was cool.

"They're both sleeping," Rick said. "Scotty could sleep through anything, I'll bet. He looks as though he didn't have a care in the world."

Chahda chuckled. "Scotty got good nerve. I guess maybe he learn how to sleep when he is a Marine."

Rick looked at the luminous dial of his watch. It was close to four o'clock. They had split the night into watches, two at a time. He and Chahda had drawn the late one.

Off the end of the peninsula, the trawler rode at anchor. An occasional glimpse of a flashlight told them that Turk's men were on watch. On the other side of the camp, the black wall of jungle was quiet. Once in a while Rick looked at it, feeling as though countless eyes were watching him. Chahda had said that the natives were watching, but they had made no move.

"We're right in the middle," Rick said. "Turk on one side and unfriendly natives on the other. Why do you suppose the natives come and go the way they've been doing? They're watching most of the time, but now and then they go away and the jungle seems to wake up."

"I think sometimes the chief is calling them together in the village to make talk," Chahda explained. "They all go see what he says, then they come back—those who watch. While they are near, the other people of this jungle, the birds and small animals, is being quiet like mouses, because they are afraid."

"Funny they haven't come back to see the dragon," Rick mused.

"True," Chahda agreed. "Maybe they not liking to have us near the dragon. They think we go away soon, then the dragon is theirs."

The dragon god had been gleaming on its pedestal in the faint moonlight, but now the sky was growing cloudy, and the darkened camp lost even the uncertain moonlight.

Rick pulled his blanket up over his shoulders. They were only a few degrees north of the Equator, but the nights were chilly and damp.

"It's the waiting that bothers me," Rick said after a moment. "I keep looking from the jungle to the ship, waiting for something to happen."

"Something happen soon," Chahda said quietly. "More natives is come."

"Are you sure?"

"Pretty sure. We just sit. Soon we find out what they want."

Rick was conscious of many eyes watching from the jungle as the minutes ticked away. He tried turning his back on the thick foliage, but that was worse. He felt better when he faced the watching eyes. It was growing lighter now, but daybreak was hidden behind massed clouds. By degrees he began to see details of the jungle. He could make out the white handkerchief strips and the trees behind them.

Then, with shocking suddenness, there was a crashing shout from the jungle! Rick leaped to his feet, Chahda beside him. Again the shout, from a hundred throats!

Something flew out of the foliage, circled high in the air and thudded to the ground before the tents.

The others were out of the tents almost instantly, waiting in silence for what might happen next. A bird cry broke the stillness, to be followed by another.

"They've gone," Scotty said. "What hit the ground out here?"

"I don't know." Rick was already walking toward the spot, his flashlight beam cutting the gloomy dawnlight. It came to rest on a carved club.

"Here it is," he called.

Gordon examined it and picked it up by the haft. It was a vicious-looking thing, a thin handle growing into a diamond-shaped head studded with shark's teeth. From the end dangled a tuft of hair. The entire head of the war club gleamed sticky red in the flashlight beam.

"Blood," Gordon said. "Probably chicken or goat blood." He looked around at the circle of faces. "We've been warned again, and by the nature of the warning, I'd say they mean business this time!"

"We'd be willing to leave," Scotty said. "If we could. Well, it's daylight. What do we do about breakfast?"

The mention of breakfast broke the atmosphere of tension the finding of the bloody club had caused. Rick thought that Scotty had known that it would. He grinned at his friend. "Come earthquake, piracy, revolution, or hurricane, that stomach of yours never stops hoping, does it?"

"It never has," Scotty returned. "Come on, let's break out that case of rations and see what gives."

The rations provided canned bacon and eggs, powdered coffee and hard biscuits, with other food for later meals. The water bag was nearly empty, but there was enough for coffee and for drinking during the day. They could wash in salt water.

As they drank the last of the coffee, the trawler stirred into life. The anchor came up and it moved out through the reef passage.

"Bet I know where they go," Chahda offered.

Scotty grinned. "It doesn't take a Hindu mystic to guess that. They're heading for the *Asamo*."

"Doubtless," Hartson Brant agreed.

Rick went with Gordon to see how Otera was getting along. The cook had regained consciousness the night before, but Gordon had given him a sedative to keep him quiet, fearing that he might have a bad concussion.

Otera woke as they changed his bandage. He tried to feel the cut on his head, but Rick held his hands. The cook poured forth a stream of *bêché-de-mer*.

"Dis fella savvy," Gordon told him. To Rick, he said, "He wanted to warn us about Turk, but he didn't dare. They had threatened to kill him. He did warn us once, but we paid no attention."

"The note," Rick exclaimed. "'Wachout Asamo!' Was that it?"

Gordon questioned Otera, then nodded. "Yes. He doesn't write very much, naturally. He got the spelling of *Asamo* from a chart Turk had. He saw it when he served dinner in Turk's cabin one day."

By the time they had finished ministering to Otera, the trawler had reached a point over the sunken ship. During the morning they watched the Submobile lowered twice, but they couldn't see whether or not it brought up anything.

"I wish I knew what Turk was planning for us," Rick complained. "This waiting is getting me down."

"He brought that mortar along for something," Scotty said.

"Obviously," Zircon replied. "Scotty, I know almost nothing about mortars. How do they work?"

"You saw the thing," Scotty began. "It looked like a big pipe set on a base plate and supported by two legs. Well, that's about all there is to it. The thing can be aimed by changing the elevation of the barrel. There's a firing table that tells you just how far a shell will travel at each angle of adjustment. The shells are miniature bombs, and they have a propelling charge in the base. There's a firing pin in the bottom of the barrel. You drop the shell in. The firing pin strikes the propelling charge and shoots it out. It explodes when it lands."

"Doesn't sound very accurate," Hartson Brant said.

"It is, though. I've seen Marine mortarmen drop shells into targets the size of pickle barrels at 1,000 yards."

Rick whistled. "That's shooting! Where do you suppose they got it?"

"That one is of Japanese make," Scotty said. "It's probably a war souvenir of Digger's."

It wasn't until after lunch that the natives returned. Scotty, watching the jungle closely, said, "I think there are only two of them. Chances are, the rest are cooking up some kind of mischief."

"I'd like to know what it is," Rick told him.

Scotty gave a wry grin. "Don't be impatient. We'll find out."

Chahda pointed at the trawler. "They dive some more."

"Not wasting any time," Gordon commented. "I wonder if they've found anything?"

"It's possible," Hartson Brant replied. "The equipment is certainly easy to operate. It was designed that way. Mallane will have no trouble unless something breaks down."

"Or unless a storm comes up," Rick added, looking at the cloudy sky.

The Submobile made two dives as they watched, then, late in the afternoon, the trawler came across the strait and through the reef. As the Spindrift party walked down to the shore, a boat was put over the side. One of the sailors took the oars, and Turk, Digger, and Hashimo got in. Two five-gallon cans were handed down to them, then the boat made for the shore, coming to a stop a few yards from the Spindrift group.

The Japanese had Scotty's rifle. Rick saw his friend's eyes harden as Scotty watched. Digger had a pistol. Turk stood up and hailed them.

"We've come to bargain."

"What do you want?" Hartson Brant asked coldly.

"We know you're short of water. We'll trade ten gallons for instructions on planting explosive charges with the Submobile."

The Spindrift group huddled together like a football squad.

"Give them some cockeyed information," Scotty suggested.

Zircon objected. "That would serve nothing. It would wreck the Submobile and perhaps do away with those in it, but it would not help us."

"True," Hartson Brant agreed. "And we do need water. We gain that much by answering Mallane and we lose nothing."

There was general agreement.

"All right," Hartson Brant told Turk. "We'll trade. Bring the water ashore."

Turk motioned them to the side of the camp away from the water bag. "Stand over there. Don't try anything or you'll get shot."

They obeyed, and watched the sailor lug the cans over and pour them into the water bag. Then Turk stepped ashore and walked over to them, stopping ten feet away.

"All right. There's your water. Now talk."

"The charges are all prepared," Hartson Brant said. "They're marked according to the size of the explosive charge in them. There are hooks on them for attaching them under water. On the side of the charge is a waterproof switch marked 'safe' and 'explode'. Clamp the charge in one of the extension arms, then throw the switch to 'explode'. Be sure the sound gear is turned off. Take it down, attach the charge by the hooks, then release the extension arm clamp and come to the surface. Turn on the sound gear and the charge will explode. The sound impulses activate a tuning fork by sympathetic vibration, and the vibrating fork closes the circuit."

Turk asked suspiciously, "Won't the Sonoscope set it off?"

"No. The sound gear sends out impulses at 30,000 cycles per second. The Sonoscope operates at 50,000. The charges are set for the sound gear."

Turk nodded. "Thanks." He turned to leave.

Hartson Brant stopped him, calling, "Just a minute, Mallane. We want to know what you intend to do with us."

Turk laughed. "Nothing. We won't lay a hand on you."

"You'll never get away with this," Zircon bellowed.

"I'd better explain," Turk said. "Just in case you think the law will ever catch up with us." He motioned toward Hashimo, who was watching their every move, the rifle pointing toward them. "He gave us the idea. You see, he was on the *Asamo* when it went down, and he was one of the survivors. There were about forty of them. They swam ashore and took over the island. The natives were friendly enough, but they didn't obey orders fast enough to suit the Japs, so the senior officer ordered his men to break the clay dragon god they worshipped. That was a piece of it you found here the first day."

"Go on," Hartson Brant said coldly. "What has this to do with us?"

"The natives were not pleased," Turk continued. "Quite the opposite. They pounced on the Japs one night and massacred the lot of them, except for Hashimo, who is an excellent swimmer. He got to Little Kwangara and was waiting there when a Jap destroyer came looking for the *Asamo*. The destroyer took him off, but it was sunk near New Guinea, and Hashimo landed in prison camp, where Digger met him."

"So you intend letting the natives do your dirty work," Gordon exclaimed. "Suppose they don't?"

"They will," Turk said calmly. "Then we'll finish getting up the treasure and sail back to Honolulu, and we'll regretfully report that you were all massacred one night here in camp. The broken radiophone will alibi us for not reporting sooner. The Navy will send out a punitive expedition, of course, but we won't mind. And you'll be past caring."

The fiendish simplicity of the plan stunned the Spindrift party. They watched, speechless, as Turk went back to the boat. He would get away with it because there would be no reason to suspect his story. He had only to explain that the scientists preferred to camp ashore, and it had caused their deaths. An investigation would show nothing!

"But it's incredible," Gordon exclaimed. "It . . . it's inhuman!"

"That doesn't seem to bother Turk," Hartson Brant said dryly.

Zircon shook his head. "History is full of tales of many more than seven persons being sacrificed for less treasure than lies out there."

Rick turned and stared at the jungle. "Why can't we do something? Maybe we could turn the dragon god over to them in exchange for our safety . . ."

"No chance," Chahda said. "Look!"

The boat had reached the trawler. Digger Sears had climbed to the deck and was carrying the mortar to an open spot on their side of the ship!

"Back to the jungle," Scotty shouted. "He's going to fire!"

"Otera!" Rick gasped. "We'll have to move him!"

He ran for the tent, Scotty, Chahda, and Zircon close behind him. They picked up the cot and carried it like a stretcher, trotting to the jungle.

"This is far enough," Gordon said as they reached the tabu line. "Drop flat, everyone."

Rick looked into the damp, jungle maze, almost a solid wall of foliage, then he looked out at the trawler. They were caught between the devil and the deep blue sea, all right. He saw Digger do something to a shell, then drop it into the barrel. There was a chugging cough as the mortar went off, silence as the shell arched high into the air, then a roar as it exploded at the water's edge, blasting coral and water into the air.

"Ranging shot," Scotty said grimly.

Not until then did Rick realize the purpose of the gunnery. Of course Turk would want no signs of shrapnel in case their bodies were found by a searching party. He was going to destroy the dragon god, to make sure the natives would carry out his plan!

The mortar coughed again, spewing out another shell. There was a pause, then the crash of the explosion.

Rick sucked in his breath. The dragon god toppled from the pedestal, a torn and twisted mass of metal!

CHAPTER XV

The Drums of Kwangara

"ANYONE hurt?" Hartson Brant called.

No one was, although a few pieces of shrapnel had hissed through the air above them. They got to their feet as the trawler got under way.

"Turk doesn't want to be too close to land, looks like," Rick said.

Chahda grinned. "Turk afraid if he stays close, maybe natives swim out to visit."

Scotty held up a warning hand. "Listen!"

There was the sound of many people crashing through the jungle foliage, and the sound was coming toward them! They picked up Otera's cot and carried it back to the tent, then faced the jungle, waiting. In a moment there were outraged cries, but no native showed himself.

"They ran at the first explosion," Gordon guessed. "Now they're just finding out that the dragon god has been wrecked."

Rick waited tensely, but although the shouts increased as the natives cried out their grief and rage, he saw none of them.

Presently the noise died and the jungle grew quiet again, but not for long. Far inland a rhythmic booming began. It was picked up from somewhere to the south, and it echoed and re-echoed until the whole island seemed to throb.

"It's coming closer," Scotty said. "Sounds like they have two or three drums in different places. They're bringing them together—here."

From the east, the roll of thunder crashed in answer to the ceremonial drums.

"Even nature is helping out," Zircon said.

Rick looked up at a sky dark with heavy clouds. It was already twilight, much earlier than usual because of the growing storm.

The throbbing drums reached a point several hundred feet away from the peninsula and came no closer. But now their deep, booming rhythm was augmented by a chant that began on a low note and gradually climbed the scale until it beat against the eardrums almost painfully.

"They're getting up steam," Gordon said. "Probably working themselves to a frenzy on palm wine and religious ceremony. They'll need to be plenty worked up before they break the tabu, but they'll do it before the night is over."

"And we've nothing to stop them," Rick said. He could visualize savage brown men pouring over the camp in an irresistible tide, their spears rising and falling. . . .

"Gentlemen," Hartson Brant said quietly, "we've long boasted that the mind always wins over force. Now, I think, we must prove it. We must put our minds to work and create a weapon. Not one of the usual sort, perhaps, not a weapon of violence."

"A weapon of science," Rick exclaimed. "But what?"

Chahda laughed. "Must be something. Would not sound good at home, if maybe papers had to say 'famous mens of science meet match in igno . . . igno-runt natives.'"

The others laughed with him, and Zircon clapped a big hand on the Hindu boy's shoulder. "We've been in tight spots before this, haven't we?"

"I propose we start by making an inventory of everything in camp," Gordon said. "Something may suggest itself."

"Good idea," Hartson Brant agreed. "Rick, you and Scotty make a list of everything in the tents. Hobart and I will look through the power equipment. Chahda can help Gordon look through the supply boxes."

"Don't miss anything," Gordon warned. "You never know what might suggest something."

The party hurried to the appointed places and rapidly went through their belongings and camping equipment. Rick took notes as Scotty dictated, and all the while he was conscious of the steady, ominous beat of the Kwangara drums. Sometimes the chanting rose to a shouting crescendo that throbbed in waves against his ears.

They took their list out to where Hartson Brant and Hobart Zircon waited, and in a moment Gordon and Chahda joined them. Rick looked from the jungle to the cloudy sky, and then out to where the trawler rode serenely 1,000 feet offshore. The trawler lights twinkled like inviting beacons. They were the only lights. The camp was growing indistinct in the waning light, and the black wall of the jungle seemed to press closer.

Hartson Brant shot a flashlight on the paper he held.

"I'll read our own list first. We have four batteries, fully charged, one gasoline-operated battery charger, one five-gallon tin of gasoline, one empty tin, about 100 feet of heavy wire, one converter, one set of tools, one water bag with ten gallons of water."

The list Rick and Scotty had compiled was mostly clothes and personal stuff. It included two jack-knives, assorted clothing, two tents with poles and steel pegs, six cots with pads and mosquito nets, four flashlights, one sledge hammer, one box of cartridges for Scotty's rifle.

Gordon and Chahda reported one case of rations, badly depleted; one electric cooking unit, one electric percolator, two first-aid and medicine kits, a pressure spray gun and a supply of powdered DDT, unused, one can of surplus fluoride powder, one ultraviolet sterilizer, both unused.

"How about shocking them?" Scotty asked. "If we could replace the tabu wire with something that carried an electric charge. . . ."

"Not practicable," Zircon said. "For two reasons. We haven't enough wire to be thorough, and if they started to rush us, only the first few would be shocked. The weight of bodies would break the wire down. No, that isn't what we're looking for, Scotty. I think we need something that will play on their superstitious fears."

"That's what I think," Gordon agreed. "Even if they're worked up to a pitch where they'll violate the tabu, they'll still be a little afraid. We must play on that fear."

Rick had been thinking of an incident during the moon rocket experiment. The paint used by the enemy gang to keep in touch with a traitor on the Spindrift

Island staff, by means of a sign on an old barn visible from the tidal flats, had been fluorescent.

"Dismal, the pup, got into the paint," Rick said aloud. "Then, under Barby's ultra-violet sun lamp, he glowed blue!"

"And scared Barby half to death," Scotty added. "Golly, Rick, maybe you've got something!"

"Hold it," Hartson Brant ordered. "Before we say any more, let's think about Rick's suggestion. We have fluoride powder and we have the ultra-violet sterilizer. How should we use them?"

Rick sat down on the ground, his legs tucked under him. He stared at the lights on the trawler and tried hard to concentrate. Behind him were the drums, throbbing endlessly. The rhythm beat around him like a tangible force, making it hard to think. If the natives broke the tabu, they should be punished . . . but punished with fluoride powder?

"All right, let's hear your ideas," Hartson Brant said.

Zircon spoke up, his voice booming out over the sound of the drums. "Could we cover ourselves with the powder, then fluoresce with the aid of the sterilizer lamp? The natives would then be confronted with a group of ghostly figures."

Gordon had an objection to that. "They'll know that it is us, of course, and I doubt we could convince them that we had suddenly turned into ghosts. They've had dealings with white men before."

"No," Hartson Brant agreed. "It must be something more spectacular than that."

"Whatever it is, it should happen to them," Rick offered. "They'll be the ones who are breaking the tabu."

"They'll break it soon," Scotty said, peering at the

dark jungle. "I wish I could get a look at what's going on."

"I also," Chahda added.

Hartson Brant said, "No, boys. We know well enough what's going on. I'm sure you could sneak over and look, but it would be a pointless risk."

"It should happen to them," Gordon mused, echoing Rick's words. "But how could we make them fluoresce?"

"Let's think of something soon," Scotty pleaded.

"Maybe we could spray with bug stuff," Chahda suggested. "Kill them like mosquito."

Zircon bellowed, "Chahda, you're a genius! Not the DDT, but the spray gun filled with fluoride!"

"Gosh, yes," Rick exclaimed. "That will blow the powder for yards. But how will we get it on them?"

"What colour will the powder be under the ultra-violet?" Hartson Brant asked.

"A yellow-green," Gordon replied. "I've seen pieces of mineral fluoride under ultra-violet. Not a pretty colour."

A drop of rain fell on Rick's nose. He looked up at the dark sky, but could only make out an occasional gleam of dying daylight. The camp was entirely dark now.

"It's starting to rain," he said. "Even the weather is against us."

"Maybe not," Scotty exclaimed. "Rain will make the powder stick better, won't it?"

The throbbing of the drums was getting faster, building up to a climax. The chanting of the natives kept pace, a low undertone of menace.

"We get company pretty soon," Chahda said. "Think quick!"

"Gordon, get the sterilizer," Hartson Brant directed. "Break open the reflector so it will throw as wide a beam as possible. Hobart, help me remove these bulbs. We want no lights when we turn the power on. Rick and Scotty, get the spray gun and the fluoride powder."

"And the tooth powder," Gordon added.

In a moment the various parts of their desperate plan were assembled. Gordon took pliers from the toolbox and wrenched the chrome-plated reflector loose, spreading it wide so that the tubular ultra-violet bulb would have the widest possible angle.

There had been so few insects in camp that the spray gun had never been filled. Rick and Scotty took off the top and were about to pour in the fluoride powder when Gordon stopped them. "The tooth powder first. We'll use a smaller concentration on the jungle before they arrive."

Chahda helped collect the half-dozen cans of powder and the jar of surplus mixture. They were emptied into the spray gun, the top replaced, then Scotty began pumping up pressure. When the air pressure was great enough, Rick swung the tank to his back and slipped into the harness. Then, with Scotty and Chahda beside him, he hurried to the edge of the jungle.

"Wait a moment," Scotty said. He slipped into the woods. Rick waited until he returned. "No natives close to us," he reported.

Rick asked curiously, "Suppose you'd met one?"

"I'd have run like crazy," Scotty replied. "Start spraying."

Rick grinned as he pressed the trigger that shot a spray of powder into the air. Scotty ran from fights the way cats run from catnip.

"Go in more," Chahda suggested.

Rick ducked under the tabu string and moved ten feet into the jungle. The leaves and fronds were always damp, because sunlight never reached to the jungle floor through the dense growth. He sprayed the area well, moving back and forth across the end of the peninsula until the tooth powder was exhausted and the spray gun was blowing air. Then they hurried back to where the scientists were at work.

His father, Zircon, and Gordon had torn down the camp lighting system and patched the wires together to form a long extension. They spliced the extension to the cord of the ultraviolet lamp, then carried the lamp toward the jungle.

There was some discussion about where to put it, and the scientists knelt, measuring angles. It was finally placed about forty feet from the jungle's edge. The radiation would be less on the edges, but that couldn't be helped.

No one had spoken aloud of how the natives were to be coated with the powder, but they all knew there was only one way. That was to spray them as they approached.

Rick looked up at the sky again. Occasional raindrops struck him, but it hadn't started raining hard as yet. It had better, he thought. Just a few raindrops wouldn't wet the natives enough so that the powder would stick to them.

"They'll get some powder on them as they push through the jungle," he said. "But we ought to really dose a few of them."

"I do that," Chahda offered.

"Nothing doing," Scotty said flatly. "I'll do it."

"We'll draw lots," Hartson Brant stated firmly.

Rick stepped to his father's side. "Not this time, Dad. Scotty, Chahda, and I will draw lots. We're better at climbing trees, and we can run a lot faster if we have to."

"Rick is right, sir," Scotty said. "We'll make a three-way draw."

"It makes sense," Rick pleaded. "You and Professor Gordon can watch the power supply and the lamp, and Professor Zircon can stand by to guard you in case they break through. He's the biggest and strongest."

"All right," Hartson Brant agreed.

"We not draw straws," Chahda suggested. "We all three go."

"I'm for it," Scotty said. "One guy alone in the woods wouldn't have a chance. But three of us might be able to fight our way out, if anything happens."

"It's settled," Rick said quickly. "What do we use for weapons?"

"Wrenches from the kit," Gordon offered.

"I know something better," Hobart Zircon said. "Those steel tent stakes."

"Let's hurry. We've got to get set before they come," Rick said. He trotted to the tent and pried out a stake. They were eighteen inches long, tapering to a point at the bottom. Toward the top, they had little metal hooks sticking out to hold the tent ropes.

Rick hefted his. Held by the pointed end, it made a wicked club. He thrust it into his belt, then carried the spray gun to where the extra can of fluoride powder waited. Scotty helped him to pour the powder in and pump up pressure, then Rick swung the tank to his back once more and secured the harness firmly.

The rain was coming down in an increasing patter of drops now, but it would have to rain harder before much penetrated the jungle foliage. He hurried to the ultra-violet lamp where the scientists had gathered.

All of them had tent stakes tucked into their belts. Scotty had two. "One to throw," he explained.

They shook hands all around, then Scotty led the way into the jungle.

"A good-sized tree, if we can locate one," he said.

Rick didn't see how they could locate anything. The jungle was pitch black. He blundered into palm fronds and hanging vines, and once he ran into a spider web that caught across his face and eyes. He clawed the thing away and hurried after Scotty. Chahda was right on his heels.

"This will do," Scotty whispered. "Up with you, Chahda. Then Rick."

By some miracle of jungle sense, Scotty had found a glade where it was comparatively clear. A tree with spreading branches was in the centre of the glade—but the branches were high above ground.

Chahda went up the trunk like a dark monkey. Rick followed, going more by feel than sight. His eyes were of little use in the almost total darkness.

"Big branch," Chahda said from above him. "Is clear space all way to ground. You get here, Rick."

Rick struggled out along the branch, the tank impeding him by catching onto smaller branches and leaves. Finally he got settled, about six feet out from the trunk, his legs dangling and his back resting against a thick branch that thrust up at an odd angle. He took the nozzle of the spray gun from its clamp and got it ready.

The rhythm of the drums seemed to swirl around them,

rising from the ground like mist. Were the natives coming, or had the drums grown louder?

"We forgot to arrange a signal for them to turn on the ultraviolet lamp," Rick whispered.

"Not forget," Chahda corrected. "While you and Scotty filling tank, I fix with Sahib Brant. When many natives go below, I give call of Siva. It tells others they come, and maybe it scares natives a little, I think."

"They'll come this way," Scotty said quietly. "There's a trail that passes under the tree."

"How can you tell?" Rick asked.

"It's a path, nothing growing on it. We'd better keep quiet now. I think they'll be along soon. Hear that chanting?"

The voices had risen to a screaming crescendo, and they were getting louder.

"What's the call of Siva?" Rick whispered to Chahda.

"Siva Hindu god. Called 'The Destroyer.' Not nice. You see."

Rick fell silent again. The patter of rain on the leaves overhead was a soft undertone to the chanting and the drums. Drops fell on his shoulders and in his hair. Good! It was raining harder!

Overhead, lightning flashed, and the jungle was lit up in blue fire for an instant. Rick saw Scotty's face beside him, and saw that they were on a thick limb about fifteen feet above the ground. Under them was a well-defined path through the forest growth.

The thunder roared in the wake of the lightning, drowning out the drums. On the heels of the reverberations came the rain, heavy now.

Inland, the drums throbbed louder and the chanting suddenly broke into rising screams and yells.

Scotty stiffened and put a hand on Rick's shoulder. "They're coming!"

Rick tensed, the nozzle trigger under his finger. He heard a crashing in the underbrush, coming nearer! And still nearer!

The lightning flashed again, and he had a quick view of wet, brown bodies and gleaming spear points. They were coming . . . they were under him!

His finger squeezed and the hiss of the pressure tank mingled with the raindrops. He moved the nozzle in wide sweeps, spreading the powder wide.

From beside him, spine-chilling in its terrible weirdness, a long wailing cry quavered, rising and falling in a cadence of terror.

The call of Siva!

CHAPTER XVI

A Two-man Boarding Party

THE rushing natives hesitated as Chahda's weird cry rang through the wet jungle. Then, as the first of them reached the tabu line, the scientists threw power into the ultra-violet lamp.

Even to Rick, who was watching for it, the effect was indescribably ghastly. The jungle lit up. Strange blotches of colour like yellow-green fire were everywhere. And the fire dripped from the leaves onto the heads of the natives! Those who had passed directly under Rick were a solid mass of yellow-green from hair to shoulders, and all of them were blotched with the stuff from where wet bodies had brushed against the foliage.

For an instant the natives were silent, shocked into stillness by the thing that had befallen them. Then Chahda's cry rang out again, followed from below by horrified gasps. From the edge of the jungle a voice babbled in the native language. It rose to a scream of pure fear that lifted the hair on Rick's head.

The hesitating natives broke and ran as though the dragon god himself had come to life! They ran in blind terror, crashing into trees, entangling themselves in vines, and as they ran they dropped their spears and clubs. Only when they passed beyond the range of the penetrating ultraviolet did their bodies cease to glow, but behind them the jungle still burned with yellow-green fire.

The boys waited until the last cries had died away toward the south of the island, then Scotty said, "Let's get out of this. I have an idea."

As one, they swung off the limb, hung by their hands and dropped to the spongy earth.

They trotted out of the jungle and found the scientists waiting. The ultraviolet lamp had been switched off, but the fluorescent glow was fading slowly. All three of the boys were coated with the powder.

"A fine-looking bunch," Gordon greeted them happily. "Did you wash in the stuff?"

"That was some performance," Hartson Brant said, putting his arm around Rick's shoulder.

"Chahda," Zircon boomed, "did that awful yell come from you?"

"Pretty good, I think." Chahda grinned. "I scare myself almost."

Scotty was waiting impatiently. "Listen," he said. "It's now or never! Do you think they saw the fluorescence from the ship?"

"No," Hartson Brant said. "It's raining hard and visibility is very poor. Look, you can barely make out the lights aboard."

"Good," Scotty said. "But they must have heard the racket. And you know what they'll be thinking!"

"That we're all dead," Rick exclaimed. "Yes! If we could only. . . ."

The others got the idea instantly.

"We can," Zircon said decisively. "Let's make our plans, quickly."

"We'll need some sort of diversion," Hartson Brant said thoughtfully. "They'll all be on deck, probably. If we had some way of making sure they'd all run to one side of the ship. . . ."

"Fire!" Chahda exclaimed.

"Explosion!" Rick said in the same breath. "The gasoline!"

"That's it," Gordon said quickly. "We can pour a little gas into the empty tin. By the time we're ready, it will have vaporized enough to explode."

"We'll need a fuse," Scotty added.

"Sure." Rick was ready with the answer. "That box of cartridges. We can break them open and lay a powder train. If we put up a tarpaulin, it won't get wet."

"Who is going?" Scotty asked.

"The best swimmers," Hartson Brant said. "Rick, Scotty, Zircon, and myself."

"How about me?" Gordon demanded hotly. "I can make it to the boat."

"Yes," Mr. Brant said soothingly, "but you know you're not as much at ease in the water as the rest of us, John, and we'll need you here to set off the explosion. Chahda is just learning to swim, so he's automatically eliminated."

"Unhappy, yes," Chahda said sadly.

"Otera is in no condition to swim," Hartson Brant continued. "Incidentally, boys, he was the one who started the rout. Did you hear him screaming? He yelled that the dragon god was sending green fire to burn them up because the tabu had been broken."

"I'll be doggoned," Rick exclaimed. "Where is he?"

"Back in bed. We let him up just long enough to do his bit. He's still pretty weak."

"Keep your voices down," Zircon cautioned. "I doubt that they can hear us, but why take chances?"

The four swimmers stripped to their shorts, then put their belts back on. Into the belts they tucked steel tent stakes. Then they walked down to the water front and stared out to where the trawler's lights shone dimly through the rain.

"How long?" Hartson Brant asked.

Scotty estimated the distance. "Twenty minutes will give us plenty of time."

"I think so, too," Rick agreed.

Zircon said, "Rick, your watch is waterproof, isn't it? Mine is, too, and we both have luminous dials. You stick with your father. Scotty will come with me. I suggest we arrive from both sides, just aft of the pilothouse."

Rick considered. From the looks, the trawler was riding stern to the island, facing into the swell. She wasn't anchored, because it was too deep out there. Probably Turk was keeping just enough way on her to hold position. There would be one man at the wheel, and he wouldn't see them if they landed just behind the pilothouse. The explosion would bring the others to the stern, to see what was happening.

Gordon joined them. "I've poured just enough gasoline into the empty can to vaporize. We'll set both cans off, however. The first will explode and the second one will burn. How do we time it?"

He checked his watch with Rick's and Zircon's.

"All right," he said. "The second hands aren't exactly together, so keep close watch. Rick, you and Hartson will board at fifteen minutes and ten seconds past the hour by your watch. Hobart, it will be fifteen and thirty-two by your watch."

They shook hands all around. Chahda appeared and said mournfully, "I start practice swimming three hour a day, you bet!"

Rick gave him a strained grin. "You can start to-morrow."

"We'll go out in single file," Hartson Brant said.

The scientist walked into the water. Rick gave him a ten-foot start, then followed. Behind came Scotty and Zircon.

It was easy swimming in the protected waters behind the reef. Outside, there would be a swell running, but not a bad one. Rick didn't worry at all about the swim. The worst moment would come when they neared the side of the ship. If anyone aboard saw them, a few well-placed shots would finish the affair.

He thought of the sharks that would certainly be outside the reef. They wouldn't bother the swimmers. They would stay well away, in fact. He had learned that sharks were cowards. But let one of the swimmers be wounded . . . the scent of blood would bring the sharks in a ravenous pack.

They neared the reef and he saw the passage, dark between the ends of coral where the sea washed in white foam. His father kept to the middle of the passage and Rick followed, swimming easily. He lifted his head and saw the trawler's lights more distinctly. She was riding the swell about 300 yards beyond the reef. But unless someone aboard decided to turn on a searchlight, they wouldn't be seen. He had trouble seeing his father's dark head only a few feet ahead of him.

F

When they were well outside the reef, Hartson Brant waited for the others to come up to him. They huddled together, treading water in the swell as the scientist gave them instructions.

"We separate here," he whispered. "Rick and I to port, Hobart and Scotty to starboard. Circle wide, in case they have a lookout. Stay in the darkness until the time comes. Then sprint for the side. Good luck."

"Good luck," the others whispered.

Rick followed as his father angled off to the left. After a few minutes he lifted his head and looked for Zircon and Scotty. They were out of sight. He settled down to a long swim.

The route led them away from the trawler, then back toward the lights in a wide circle. Rick could see the lights winking through the rain, but he could make out no other features. And, with the hiss of the rain striking the water, even the sound of the engines was muffled.

He held his watch close to his eyes and wiped the crystal. It was twelve minutes past the hour. He increased his stroke and came up with his father.

"Three minutes more," he whispered.

"We'll start in," the scientist whispered back. His face was a white blur, but Rick thought that he smiled. "Frightened, son?"

Rick grinned back. "Scared stiff," he answered, with perfect truth. But he knew from past experience that his fright would vanish in the heat of the fight. Scotty was like that, too. He had always told Rick that the minutes before the battle were the worst.

"Don't pull your punches," Mr. Brant warned in a whisper. "We can't afford to lose. Tap me on the shoulder when we've exactly one minute. No more talk."

He squeezed Rick's shoulder, then resumed swimming, straight for the side of the trawler. Rick followed, careful not to splash as they neared the ship. He could make out details now: the high bulk of the pilothouse and the rest of the superstructure, the gleam of light on the Submobile. Once he thought he heard voices.

They moved close enough so that Rick could see clearly. The ship was well lit, working lights aft. He could make out figures there, and thought he recognized Turk's broad shoulders. He started to tread water as Hartson Brant stopped just outside the fan of light from the ship.

He glanced at his watch, counted off the seconds, then tapped his father on the shoulder. The scientist nodded. Rick loosened the tent stake in his belt a bit.

When he glanced at his watch again, holding it close to his eyes, there were only twenty seconds remaining. He looked toward the dark shore and counted under his breath. His heart was pounding and nervousness was making him a little short of breath.

An explosion split the night and yellow flame shot high in the air!

Hartson Brant was face down in the water, his arms moving in a powerful crawl before Rick could get started. Then he put his head down and sprinted, going as fast as he could without splashing.

The scientist gained the side of the ship, reached far up and caught hold, then pulled himself over the side. Rick was right behind him. He dropped to the deck as his father started aft, and then whirled suddenly as some instinct warned him.

The sailor in the pilothouse was looking right at him, his mouth open to yell!

CHAPTER XVII

Recapture of the "Tarpon"

RICK jerked the steel tent stake from his belt and lifted it to throw, but another was there before him. There was a dull thud as a stake crashed down on the sailor's head, and arms caught him as he fell.

Scotty stepped out of the pilothouse. "Let's go," he called softly, already moving.

It had taken only a fraction of a second. Hartson Brant was not yet past the galley door. Rick and Scotty ran after him, noiseless in their bare feet. As they reached the afterdeck, Zircon came around the other side, a huge, terrible figure of vengeance with tent stake held high.

The enemy was clustered at the after rail, the Submobile shielding the swimmers from them. As the boarders rounded the shining, undersea craft Rick saw Turk Mallane, his back to them, leaning on the rail.

"Looks like the natives got to playing with matches," Turk said. He laughed. Then, sensing something, he whirled.

"Not the natives," Rick said, and his tent stake was already swishing down in a vicious arc. His hand stung as the weapon caught the captain squarely on the forehead.

164

Turk's mouth opened and his eyes glazed. He had a look of astonishment on his swarthy face as he slumped to the deck.

Out of the corner of his eye Rick saw one of the sailors go down as his father swung, and saw Zircon's stake raised over Digger's head. Then the other sailor was leaping for him. Rick jumped back, but the slippery footing betrayed him. He fell, the sailor on top of him.

The hand with the tent stake was free. Rick reversed ends and pushed upward with all his strength just as a fist caught him behind the ear. The sailor gave a moan and drew away for a second. Rick writhed free and started to swing, but it was not necessary. The sailor was lifted bodily. Hobart Zircon whirled him high overhead, then threw him into the side of the Sub-mobile. He slid in a limp heap to the deck.

Rick jumped to his feet and took in the situation at a glance.

Turk, the two sailors, and Digger Sears were sprawled on the deck. The mate had a cut on his temple, but he was still breathing. Hartson Brant and Hobart Zircon were running to help Scotty who was locked with Hashimo on the deck.

Rick hurried to help, too, his tent stake ready, but Scotty gasped, "Keep out of this!"

The two scientists stopped and Rick tucked the tent stake back into his belt. The Japanese stowaway had thrown Scotty the night they discovered him. Then, during the mutiny, he had acquired Scotty's beloved rifle, and he had kicked him.

Rick knew that Scotty had been fuming inside, even though his friend hadn't said much. Scotty wouldn't want any help in taking care of the Jap.

The two on the deck were tied up in a knot, and the Jap had Scotty in a punishing hold. But Scotty gave a sudden heave, bringing his open hand down sharply on the side of his enemy's neck. Hashimo flinched and Scotty pulled free.

In an instant they were on their feet, crouched low, facing each other. They were bent almost double at the waist, arms hanging loose, slightly bent at the elbows. They circled like two wary cats.

Rick understood, although he had never seen anything like it before. This was judo, "the gentle art," the most brutal scientific method of fighting in the world.

The Jap lunged suddenly, his face contorted. Scotty's arm flashed up, and the side of his hand caught Hashimo under the nose. Hashimo shook his head and started to back up, then with amazing speed, he threw his whole body forward, hands outstretched. He caught Scotty, and the weight of his body shifted. Scotty went into the air, arching backward. By some miracle of agility he made a catlike twist and landed on his feet, his knees bending for an instant, then they straightened out like steel springs as Scotty jumped forward.

Hashimo sprang to meet the charge, hands ready to break a judo hold. But Scotty surprised him. A fist brushed aside Hashimo's defence like a battering ram and the other fist described a short arc that ended flush against the broken nose.

The Japanese rocked backward with a cry of pain, then his body curved in mid-air as he jumped feet first. Scotty leaped aside and his hand chopped down. Hashimo crashed to the deck.

Scotty waited until his adversary was on his feet, then he stepped in, swinging.

Hashimo was no mean boxer. He tried hard, and he landed blows on Scotty's face and body with the side of his open hand, hardened in the Japanese fashion by breaking boards with it. But for every blow he sent home, he took three or four. Both his eyes were black, and his cheek was bleeding. He staggered and his guard dropped. Scotty smashed home a short chop with all of his powerful shoulder behind it. Hashimo's knees came unhinged. They buckled and he swayed. Then he fell face down on the deck and didn't stir again.

Rick suddenly realized where they were, and why. "Holy smoke," he exclaimed, "there's no one steering!" He sprinted for the pilothouse just as the sailor Scotty had knocked out began to stir.

There wasn't time to be merciful. Rick tapped the sailor with his tent stake. The sailor went to sleep again.

The wheel was swinging free. Rick took it, noting that there was still a dim glow from the gasoline fire ashore. He took his bearings on that and straightened the ship out. Then he found the button for the air horn and pushed it, three short blasts and a long one.

V for Victory! Gordon, Chahda, and Otera would hear it and know. He locked the wheel in place, then ran back to see what was going on. The others had cut up lengths of rope and were just finishing tying up the late mutineers.

Seeing that everything was under control, he ran back to the pilothouse. Scotty joined him in a moment, and he was grinning.

"Now I can look Chahda in the face again," Scotty said with satisfaction.

Rick laughed. "We all can. We took them completely by surprise."

"A good thing," Scotty said. He rubbed a bruise on his cheek. "Our Oriental pal was no softy. For a while I thought he was going to open me up like a melon."

"He didn't have a chance," Rick said. "You had him on the run from the time you started."

Hartson Brant came into the pilothouse. "Doing all right, Rick? I wonder if we dare run the reef passage at night."

Rick looked out at the rain-swept sea. "I don't think so, Dad," he said doubtfully. "It would be better to take a small boat in for the others."

"You're right," the scientist agreed. "Want to come with me, Scotty? Rick can stay at the wheel while Hobart keeps an eye on our friends." He smiled. "Incidentally, that was an excellent demonstration you put on. Congratulations."

Scotty turned red. "Thank you, sir. Shouldn't we get started right away? The others will be anxious to know what happened."

"Let's go," Hartson Brant agreed.

A cool, sunny morning dawned on a strange sight. All hands aboard the trawler were eating breakfast, with the exception of Gordon, who was taking his turn at the wheel, and Otera, who was asleep in a bunk.

Rick, Scotty, Chahda, Zircon, and Mr. Brant were eating on the hatch cover, and complimenting Scotty on his surprising ability as a cooker of ham and eggs. Rick came in for his share of praise as a coffee maker.

However, the Spindrift party dined with two pistols very prominent as table centrepieces, and Scotty's rifle leaned against his leg.

The prisoners were eating, but not in such comfort.

They were backed up to the after rail, seated on the deck. Their hands were free, to permit them to eat, but nooses around their necks secured them to the top rail. This was Chahda's development. The nooses were not tight enough to hurt, or to interfere with eating, and they were all connected by a trip wire which in turn was connected to a suspended small anchor. The ingenious arrangement made it safe to untie the prisoners' hands. If they tried to move more than a few inches, the nooses would tighten. If they tried to untie themselves, the tugs necessary to undo the tight knots would trip the anchor and leave the lot of them strangling until someone rescued them.

Over breakfast coffee, Hartson Brant called a council of war.

"In spite of our difficulties, I am not disposed to call the expedition off," the scientist said. "We're safe from the natives while we're aboard ship, and we have enough hands to continue our dives. All of us have operated boats before, and if we remember this is only a larger version, we'll have no difficulty. Gordon will be captain, since he can navigate. We'll all bear a hand with the engines, if they need attention."

"How about our prisoners?" Scotty asked. "There's no jail aboard and we can't keep them tied up all the time."

"I have the answer to that, too," Hartson Brant said. He pointed to where Little Kwangara thrust out of the sea.

"Like Crusoe Robin," Chahda said. "We maroon them."

"I suggest that we leave them there when we're through diving," Zircon stated. "We can make our way

to Guam, which is the closest Navy base, and tell our
tale to the commandant. I'm sure the Navy will be glad
to send a destroyer to take them off."

Rick nodded agreement. He asked, "But do we make
all our dives at the temple?"

The others laughed.

"Got the treasure bug, Rick?" his father smiled.
"Turk has some very interesting charts and diagrams
that I want to study. Yes, I think we might take a look
at the treasure ship later today. Unless someone dis-
agrees, of course."

No one did.

CHAPTER XVIII

The Treasure Ship

RICK was getting nervous. The Submobile had been on the bottom an awfully long time, and standing in the pilothouse, he couldn't keep track of what was going on.

Through the window he could see the rocky pile that was Little Kwangara. There were a few palms around the shore, but it was largely rock. A thread of smoke wound up through the feathery palm tops and he knew that Turk and Company had a fire going, probably to cook their rations.

The sound of the winch signalled the rise of the Submobile and Rick heaved a sigh of relief. At least he didn't have to worry any more about his father and Gordon. But what had they found on the bottom? He waited until he heard the Submobile swing on board, then he turned the trawler past Little Kwangara and headed her out into the open sea. He locked the wheel in position, throttled down, and hurried back to see what had happened.

The others were already gathered around the charts spread out on the hatch, and Hartson Brant was explaining what they had found.

"The ship is on her starboard side, pretty much intact except for the torpedo holes. Now, according to Turk's diagram of the superstructure, the treasure room is also on the starboard side, behind a gun turret."

He made a quick sketch of the *Asamo's* position. She was on her side, resting at about a thirty-degree angle. The treasure room was on the *under* part of the superstructure.

"Turk wanted information on setting explosive charges," Gordon said. "He must have come to the same conclusion that we did. The only chance of getting the treasure out is to plant charges under the superstructure and blow the walls out. Then, if we're lucky, the treasure chests will fall clear and we can pick them up."

"But how are you going to get underneath to plant the charges?" Scotty objected.

Mr. Brant smiled mirthlessly. "That, Scotty, is the problem. There's room enough for the Submobile to go in, but we mustn't forget that our lives depend on the cable. To get under the superstructure, the cable would have to make a sharp turn, resting against the edge of the deck. The question is, is it worth the risk?"

"If the cable got fouled. . . ." Rick didn't complete the thought.

Hartson Brant walked to the rail and stared out over the side. Rick watched him, knowing that it was a difficult decision to make. His father had never shied away from risks, but he had always told Rick, "Before you take a risk, always do a little figuring. Is the result worth the hazard?"

The others were watching Mr. Brant, too, waiting for him to decide.

Presently the scientist turned from the rail and motioned them to gather around him.

"As a research scientist," he said, "I shouldn't be influenced by any consideration of money, but I must admit that I am." He smiled at them. "Let's be practical. You know that there is never enough money for scientific research. Our own treasury is getting low, since we turn our experiment results over to the public without profit, and we have a number of expensive projects coming up. The Pacific Ethnographic Society is in a similar position."

"It's a point to consider," Zircon agreed. "Since we never try to make money from our developments, we must get capital from some source. You think it's worth the risk, Hartson?"

"We'll eliminate as much of the risk as possible, Hobart, by a careful survey of the ship. Then we'll make one trial effort. If the risk is still great, we'll abandon the project."

Rick looked at his watch. "There's time for another long dive today, Dad."

Hartson Brant nodded. "We'll go together, Rick."

The ship stirred into activity. The oxygen bottles were replaced with full ones, giving a ten-hour supply. The cable connections were examined carefully. Then Rick aided his father in securing the explosive charges. There were two of them to be taken down, one for each salvage arm. From the outside they looked like metal boxes covered with hooks, but inside was a complicated arrangement that included batteries and electronic equipment for translating the sound impulses into the electric current that would explode the charge.

As they finished locking the charges into the arm clamps, Hobart Zircon came aft. "We're standing fifteen feet away from the top of the ship, centred on the super-structure, as nearly as I can gauge it," he said.

"Good." Hartson Brant folded the ship diagrams under his arm. "Ready, Rick?"

They got in, tested equipment and phones, then settled themselves for the ride down. At 700 feet, the Submobile came to a stop. Rick switched on the Sonoscope and the searchlight, but nothing showed either on the screen or through the observation port.

The Submobile began to descend again, slowly and smoothly. Scotty was operating the winch. Chahda was working furiously with the clamps, aided now and then by Zircon, who had an extension line on his phone set.

A faint signal appeared on the Sonoscope screen. Rick tried to focus, but the outline was too vague. He leaned over and looked through the observation port, and saw why. They were near the big radar antenna on the ship's tallest mast. The outlines of the thin metal pieces were too slender to register well.

"Let's check our position," Hartson Brant said. He opened the charts he had brought. One was a side view of the ship, another was a sketch of the treasure room, showing four large trunks and a safe. He marked their position, off the tip of the forward mast, then phoned to the deck. "Take us aft, about fifteen feet. No, don't take us up. We're clear of the ship."

It was a good fifteen minutes before the Submobile stopped swaying on its cable. Then Rick looked at the Sonoscope screen and tried to focus. "We're too high," he said. "Let's go down ten feet."

Mr. Brant gave the order and the Submobile descended. The Sonoscope focused on a shelf of solid metal that ended halfway down the screen. Under the shelf, the screen went out of focus, showing that the space went far back.

"We're at the top edge of the superstructure," Mr. Brant said. "I'll move us closer and you can see through the observation port."

Rick tried to pierce the gloom past the searchlight beam as the Submobile swung in, driven by the after propeller. He began to make out details. The solid colour on the Sonoscope was the upper deck. The sharp tilt of the deck made it appear that the Submobile was suspended nose down in space, pointing at the roof edge of a high building. "Close enough," he called. "Now what?"

"Let's go down ten feet," Hartson Brant ordered. "But very slowly."

The picture on the screen changed, and Rick was suddenly looking at three great pipes that thrust up into the bottom edge of the Sonoscope. Hartson Brant ordered another ten feet of depth, and the picture became clear. They were guns, not pipes.

The position was confusing, since the ship was on its side. Rick's view was the same as if he had been hanging head down, looking at the top of the turret.

"We're right where we want to be," Hartson Brant said. "Do some figuring, Rick. The treasure room is right above those guns. If we blast it open, what happens?"

Rick puzzled over the picture of the turret. "Well, the turret has a sharp slant. If the treasure chests drop on it, they'll slide off, probably, and either get caught on the gun barrels or slide to the bottom."

Hartson Brant nodded agreement. "In either case, we could pick them up. Now, what could the cable catch on?"

Rick looked through the observation port. "I can't see anything. We should go back up, until we're above the ship. Then we can watch everything we pass on the way down."

"I agree." Hartson Brant ordered, "Take us up to 700 and hold."

Rick grinned. He knew his father was a step ahead of him all the way, but the scientist was letting him do the talking, making him puzzle out the problem as they went.

Once back at 700 feet, they started to descend again. As they went, Hartson Brant kept the side propellers going, swinging the nose from side to side. There were no major obstructions that might catch the cable. They reached the lower edge of the deck and the Submobile halted, at an order to the trawler.

"Well," Hartson Brant said calmly, "do we try it?"

Rick looked at the Sonoscope screen and gave a little shiver. They had to use full propeller power, to swing like a Yo-yo at the end of its string, figuring their arc so that it would miss the turret, ending up at the angle where the deck of the ship met the wall of the super-structure. They would have to drive in about twenty-five feet from freedom, dragging their cable against the edge of the roof as they went.

And they were more than 100 fathoms under, with tremendous pressure on them. The smallest break in the Submobile's armour. . . .

"Let's give it a whirl," Rick said, and his voice sur-prised him by being steady.

Hartson Brant spoke crisp orders into the phone. "We're going in. Give us cable very slowly, and be ready for anything I might say."

Zircon's voice was tense in the earphones. "Right. We're on our toes."

"Ten feet," the scientist ordered. Then, as the Submobile began to sink, he threw power into the aft propeller. Rick was holding the Sonoscope focusing knobs so tightly that his hands shook.

Suddenly a rasping screech sent an icy wave through him. The cable was scraping on the edge of the roof. The Submobile came to a halt, shuddering under the propeller drive. The rasping stopped.

"Another ten feet," Hartson Brant ordered. "We're under the overhang."

Rick focused on the angle where the deck met the wall. Then he looked out through the observation port. The searchlight showed the angle dimly. They still had a distance to go. The Submobile began to move again.

"Watch upward," Hartson Brant said. "Get forward as far as you can. Look for a porthole."

Rick did, and saw that they were only a few feet under the wall. The strain on the cable must be tremendous. It ran down from the ship and turned the corner, a sharp angle. If it broke . . . but it wouldn't. It could take more than they were giving it. It had been specially made. It wouldn't break—he hoped!

He saw a circle in the smooth surface overhead and called, "Porthole!"

"How far are we from the deck?"

He sighted. "Close enough! Hold it, Dad, hold us right here!" The deck angle was only about six feet away.

Hartson Brant had the most difficult task, holding the shuddering Submobile in position with just the right amount of power in the aft propeller.

Rick pressed his face against the observation port and looked for a break in the smooth deck, or in the wall. In a moment he saw just the thing . . . a cleat on the deck, right at the angle. He was cool as an ice cube now. He took the pistol grip that controlled the left extension arm and moved it forward, the explosive charge at its tip. Now to engage a hook in the deck cleat. The explosive charge blocked his view. He moved it into place until he felt the electric motor change tone as it pushed the charge against the deck. Then he lifted it, let it slide down. It stopped sliding! He put pressure downward on the extension arm and the motor whined again. It was caught! He released the arm clamp, and the explosive charge hung secure on the cleat!

Hartson Brant gave an audible sigh. "Wipe your forehead, Rick. You're melting."

Rick mopped his face. He hadn't even noticed the sweat running off his nose. "Dad, we'll have to back up about three feet."

"Right, son. Here we go." Hartson Brant slowed the aft propeller a little at a time and the Submobile swung slightly down away from the overhead wall and back just enough.

Rick took the control for the extension arm he had just used to place the charge. He moved it up and out, right at the black circle of the porthole. It reached it, and kept on going. The blackness was only water. He had been afraid it was a steel covering.

It was easy after that. He retracted the left arm and took the control for the right one, which held the second charge. It was only a matter of pushing the charge through the open port and releasing it. He pushed the arm far enough through the porthole so that the charge wouldn't drop out again. He released the clamp and withdrew the arm, slowly. Then he gave a sigh of relief. The charge was in the room!

Now, if they could get safely out again. . . .

That was Hartson Brant's problem. If he asked for too much cable, they would swing down and strike the turret. He slowed the aft propeller, letting the Submobile drift down and back a few feet, then he speeded the motor again and held it there.

"Take up five feet of slack," he ordered. "No more."

The cable rasped, sending a shiver through Rick again. It was horribly loud in the Submobile. The process was repeated, twice, three times. And the last time, they hung free again, the edge of the upper deck visible in the screen.

Father and son shook hands solemnly and grinned their relief.

"Take us up," Hartson Brant ordered. "The charges are in place!"

CHAPTER XIX

The Last Dive

WILLING hands helped Rick and Hartson Brant to the deck, and Otera, a bandage startlingly white against the inky black of his hair, arrived in person to pour fresh coffee.

They sat down on the hatch, weaker than they had realized from the strain of the trip, and described the adventure in detail.

Scotty put his arm around Rick's shoulder. "Old son, when I saw the cable vibrate, I almost passed out. I thought you were a cooked goose for fair!"

"I thought so myself." Rick grinned. "Any grey hair in my head?"

Chahda's brown skin was still unnaturally white. "In all my life I am never so fright. I think 'Oh, unhappy day! Now these good friends is become some statistics for the Worrold Alm-in-ack!'"

"If the explosive charges fail to do the job," Zircon bellowed, "I say to tophet with the treasure! Let it stay on the bottom."

"Amen," Gordon said. "When do we explode the charges?"

Hartson Brant finished his coffee and rose. "Right now."

Gordon went back to the pilothouse and swung the trawler around, heading once more for Little Kwangara. Just off the tip, a 1,000 yards away from the sunken *Asamo*, he stopped the ship. Hobart Zircon reconnected the sound gear.

"Here she goes," the big scientist shouted. He threw the switch that sent forth the sound impulses.

There was silence as they waited, then the trawler shuddered. Over the *Asamo*, huge bubbles broke the surface.

"Now," Hartson Brant said, smiling, "we run for the open sea to spend the night, since we don't dare anchor off either of these islands—thanks to our enemies. During the night the turmoil down below will settle. And tomorrow . . . well, we'll just have to go down and see what's happened."

It was still dark when Rick awoke. In spite of a small amount of sleep—he had taken his two-hour watch at midnight—the excitement of the treasure hunt had wakened him before dawn. Scotty was on watch, but Chahda was in his bunk.

"You wake, too?" Chahda asked.

"Yes," Rick said. "Go on back to sleep. It's the middle of the night."

"Look who talks." Chahda chuckled. "Go back to sleep yourself."

"I can't," Rick said. "Let's go topside. It's almost time to get up anyway."

Hartson Brant was having coffee in the galley. He looked at them in surprise, then laughed. "You two got the get-up urge, too, I see. Well, you're the last. Gordon and Zircon are in the pilothouse with Scotty. Otera is the only sleepyhead."

They had a quick breakfast then went forward. To the east, a thin sliver of salmon-pink sky heralded the dawn. Scotty, Zircon, and Gordon were lazily watching it.

"Who goes down?" Chahda asked.

"Gordon and I reached a decision by the unscientific method of flipping a coin," Zircon boomed. "He won. Scotty will go with him."

Rick felt a stir of disappointment. He had hoped to go again himself.

Gordon saw his disgruntled expression. "You stay on deck, Rick. And your father, too. We're splitting the risks as evenly as possible. Hobart and Chahda will make the second dive of the day. If there's a third, you can go again."

It was the fairest way, of course. But Rick would have liked to continue the work they had started yesterday.

They chatted until the daylight had spread in a wide fan over the eastern half of the sky, then Scotty swung the trawler around and headed back to Kwangara. The others went aft and began getting the Submobile ready.

It was full daylight before they were finished. Hobart Zircon manned the sound gear and located them as close to yesterday's position as possible, calling out directions to Gordon, who had taken the wheel. When the trawler finally rode over the selected spot, Zircon took the wheel, while Hartson Brant handled the winch. Rick put on the earphones, and Chahda stood by to clamp cable.

The Submobile, with Gordon and Scotty, went over the side and came to rest at 700 feet. Scotty reported as Gordon turned on the Sonoscope and requested additional depth.

"What's happening?" Rick asked.

"We're taking a look," Scotty answered. "The bottom of the superstructure opened up like a sardine can. Wait. . . . Take us down five feet."

"Five feet down," Rick called to his father, who was handling the winch.

"It's murky," Scotty's voice came up the phone line. "The bottom is still stirred up. We're depending on the Sonoscope. Stand by."

The minutes ticked away, then Scotty's voice came again, but it didn't sound like Scotty. He was breathless with excitement. "Two chests lying on the turret!"

Chahda ran to tell Zircon. Rick held tight to the mouthpiece and waited. Far below, Gordon and Scotty were looking around, trying to locate other chests that might have fallen. Once they asked for more cable and brought the Submobile to rest on the bottom.

"Only the two," Scotty reported. "Getting them is going to be tough. Stand by."

The minutes dragged. Now and then the whine of the generator indicated the use of power down below. Rick looked over the side into the green depths and started biting his nails. He wanted to open the circuit and demand information, but he knew he shouldn't disturb the work on the bottom.

"Okay," Scotty reported at last. "We snared one chest in the salvage cable, and we got a grip on it with the scoop. Reel in the salvage cable while you bring us up, but be careful not to put too much tension on it."

Rick relayed the orders to Hartson Brant. The scientist shook his head. "This is going to be tough. Chahda, put the phones on and plug in the extension. You'll have to listen while you unclamp the cable. Rick, take over the salvage cable winch. Watch your footage meter. I'll read mine aloud, and it's up to you to keep them together. Too much tension on yours will pull the chest loose. Too little will put its entire weight on the scoop. So keep on your toes."

Rick took a grip on the handle that controlled the electric winch motor. "Ready," he said.

It was delicate work, keeping the two cables coming at the same rate of speed. By the time the Submobile broke the surface, he was limp. They brought the under-sea craft up almost to the booms, then locked the winches and hurried to help with the boom ropes. The Submobile was swung inboard, then they hurried back to the winches and lowered it to the deck. Clasped firmly in the jaws of the scoop, the salvage cable tight around it, was a rusted steel chest!

Gordon and Scotty dropped to the deck as Rick swung the hatch away, then they all gathered around the chest. Zircon set a course for the open sea, so that he need not watch the wheel, and hurried back. The chest was released from the Submobile and lowered to the deck.

"What's in it?" Rick asked breathlessly.

"We'll soon find out," Gordon stated. He and Chahda hurried below decks and came up with cold chisels and heavy hammers. In a moment the deck rang with the pounding as the rusted hinges were cut away.

"Now," Hartson Brant said. He took a pinch bar and inserted it under the lid. He threw his weight on it, and water poured out. The cover flew off.

They bent over a mass of soggy, bleached paper!

Rick looked at the others, his disappointment plain on his face. "Nothing! Nothing but a lot of wet paper!"

Hartson Brant peeled off a thin sheet of the soggy stuff and held it to the light. "Wet paper, eh? This piece I have is an English ten-pound note! This is the paper money chest!"

"But is all spoiled," Chahda declared.

"The experts won't think so," Gordon said solemnly. "They'll go through this stuff with their special equipment, and they'll get the number and amount and country of each bill, and their findings will be accepted at face value."

Even Zircon's booming voice was hushed. "It's impossible to make an estimate, but I'll wager that chest represents more than a million dollars!"

Rick stared at the soggy mass in disbelief. It had to be true if the scientists said it was, but it was hard to believe. "I hope there's something that looks more like treasure in the other box," he declared.

Gordon nodded. "Because that other one is the last one we'll get."

Rick looked up in surprise. "Aren't we going after the rest?"

"I'm afraid not," Gordon said. "The blast curled the steel down like a sharp blade. We couldn't get close enough to plant charges. We'll have to be content with the two chests."

"What we wait for?" Chahda asked eagerly. "Why we not go now for the other?"

"Why not?" Zircon echoed. "Let's stow this one below decks and go after that other chest!"

Willing hands busied themselves with the details of

the dive and the Submobile was on its way to the bottom again within a half hour. This time Zircon and Chahda were in the undersea craft. Rick was at the phones, his father at the winch, and Scotty stood by to clamp cable with the aid of Otera. Gordon was at the wheel.

"You're at 700," Rick told Chahda, at his father's signal. He looked past the winch toward Little Kwangara and noticed a drifting tree, green branches in the air.

"Take them down ten feet," he repeated as Chahda phoned instructions. He turned and watched Scotty put on another clamp, securing the power line to the main cable. Suddenly he whirled. Something had just registered. The tree! *It had been moving against the swell!*

He started to jerk off the phones, then realized that he shouldn't. "Scotty!" he yelled. "That tree! Turk!"

Scotty's quick wits needed no detailed picture. He dropped the last clamp and jumped for his rifle. Another leap took him to the rail, the rifle already at his shoulder.

The eight rounds of the clip went off like a machine gun as Scotty triggered. Rick, holding his position but straining to see, saw the foliage fly and the smaller branches droop. Suddenly three heads were bobbing in the water, heading for Little Kwangara as fast as arms could pull them through the swell.

Scotty slapped another clip into his rifle. He took careful aim this time. The rifle barked and a spurt of water shot up not more than two inches from the nearest head. Scotty triggered again and again, the shots landing so close that water sometimes spurted into the faces of the swimmers. Not until they had reached the reef of the little island did he reload and put his rifle down.

"I didn't try to hit them," he said, laughing. "I just tried to make good citizens out of 'em. They won't be back for a while."

"Turk, Hashimo, and Sears," Rick said. "Gosh! I almost didn't notice."

"But you did," Hartson Brant said. "That's the important thing. Good shooting, Scotty. They'll think twice about trying that again."

"They must have figured we'd be too busy with the dive to notice," Rick said. "They figured right, too. It was just luck that I saw them." He broke off suddenly as Chahda phoned up. "Right. Give them ten feet more, Dad."

Gordon and Scotty had taken the larger and more difficult chest first. The one Zircon and Chahda snared had two brass handles that gave a purchase to the salvage cable. There was no difficulty in bringing it to the surface.

In a short while the hammers and chisels were at work again, breaking the hinges from the chest.

Chahda broke the cover off and exposed a number of soggy boxes made of what had once been pressed board. He picked one up, and it fell apart in his hands.

The others gasped in unison as crimson fire flashed from the pebbles that fell to the deck. Rubies! A fortune in rubies! They were damaged somewhat, but the surfaces could be polished, restoring them to full lustre. In silence they opened another of the soggy boxes and exposed a mound of golden rings, from which diamonds sparkled.

Before them lay the loot of the Indies, Singapore, and Hong Kong; valuables taken from prisoners and refugees, found in vaults, or stolen from private homes by the conquerors. The Spindrift party gazed in silence as Chahda uncovered fortune after fortune in brooches, unset stones, uncut emeralds, pearls, and necklaces.

It was Scotty who finally put into words what was in all their minds.

"Let the fish have the other chests. Why, we've got half the treasure in the whole world right here!"

CHAPTER XX

Homeward Bound

SCOTTY, Rick, and his sister Barby were stretched out on the sand in front of the Lehua Hotel. Chahda, who was determined to become the world's best swimmer if he drowned in the attempt, was making the water foam a few feet offshore.

Barby, a slim, brown water sprite after a month in the Hawaiian sun, remarked, "That dragon you brought back is the ugliest thing I've ever seen. I don't see why Dr. Warren got so excited."

"Neither do I," Scotty agreed. "But I wish we could have brought back the other one. It would have looked nice on the Spindrift boat landing. Salesmen would run a mile when they saw it."

The dragon was a souvenir of their last days at Kwangara. A few more days of diving at the temple had netted two dragons, almost three. Gordon thought that there had been four, originally, one at each corner of the temple. The first had been destroyed by Sears and Turk. The second was safely delivered to the Pacific Ethnographic Society. The third had slipped from the salvage cable and had fallen to the bottom. The fourth —that had been Chahda's idea. They had taken it to

Camp Spindrift, and Otera had made a speech to the unseen watchers.

"We are your friends," he declared in the Polynesian dialect of the island. "All strangers who come to your island from now on must be treated as friends. See, we have returned your dragon god. The tabu is lifted!"

More of the temple frieze had been brought up, and added to the pieces they already had. Dr. Warren, delighted beyond words, had already put his staff to work.

"It was rough going for a while," Rick said lazily, "but I guess the expedition was worth it."

"You guess!" Barby said indignantly. "After finding all that treasure!" Her voice got wistful. "I sort of wish you could have kept just one little tiny emerald for me. I love emeralds."

"Wait until we get the Spindrift share," Scotty smiled. "We'll buy you a dozen of 'em."

"That won't be for a long while," Rick said. The treasure was an international problem, since Dutch, French, English, Australian, Chinese, and American ports or persons had been robbed to accumulate it. It had been turned over to the Navy at Guam for safe-keeping while the governments got together. But international salvage agreements insured a good share for the scientific groups.

The Navy had been most co-operative. A destroyer had been sent for Turk and his gang, and the Guam base commander had found a way around service regulations to lend the Spindrift party an officer and four sailors to see the trawler safely back to Honolulu.

"Turk and the rest must be in the States by now," Rick said, a little enviously. He was anxious to get back to Spindrift again.

"Must be," Scotty agreed. "The Navy commander said he'd put them on a service plane, under guard, and turn them over to the Federal authorities at San Francisco."

"There's a lot you've never told me," Barby said resentfully. "I can tell when you're holding out! What really happened, Rick?"

"Not much," Rick said carelessly. "Turk Mallane tried to take over the ship and we wouldn't let him. Then we put him and his pals ashore so we wouldn't have any trouble with them. That's all."

"Never mind," Barby said. "I'll get it out of you one of these days."

"You probably will," Rick agreed. "You can wheedle the flowers off the wallpaper when you put your mind to it. But if Mom ever finds out . . . she'd never let us out of her sight again."

Chahda stood over them dripping wet. He said, "You want to know what happens, Barby? Ask Chahda. He tells all."

Barby sat up eagerly. "Will you? What happened, Chahda?"

Chahda looked around to make sure no one was within hearing distance. He leaned close and his voice got confidential. "We was captured by cannibals."

Barby's eyes got round and horrified. "No!"

"Yes," Chahda said solemnly. "And is not all." His voice sank still lower. "We was boiled and eaten—with ketchup."

Barby's retaliation was swift. She grabbed Chahda's ankles and pulled. The Hindu boy went over backward and landed with his head in the foam.

Rick and Scotty laughed as he came up spluttering.

Mrs. Brant came down the path and smiled down at them. "Isn't it time you started dressing? Be sure to wear your white suits, boys. Remember this dinner is as much in your honour as anyone's."

"That's the trouble with being famous," Rick groaned. "You always have to dress up for it."

"Your father got a letter," Mrs. Brant said. "From Julius Weiss."

Rick sat upright. "Honest? What did he say?" He knew his mother wouldn't have mentioned it unless it were important.

"I think we'll be leaving for home shortly," Mrs. Brant said. "He mentioned something about a new experiment."

"Where is Dad?" Rick asked eagerly.

"In the cottage," Mrs. Brant replied.

Rick was on the sea wall in one leap, Scotty right beside him. "Mom, do you remember anything about the experiment? What kind? Is it another expedition, or is it at home?"

Mrs. Brant shook her head, laughing. "You'd better talk to your father."

Rick and Scotty didn't even wait for her to finish. They were sprinting up the path as fast as they could run!